The Stranger's Message

The Stranger's Message

Paul McCusker

PUBLISHING
Colorado Springs, Colorado

THE STRANGER'S MESSAGE

Library of Congress Cataloging-in-Publication Data
McCusker, Paul, 1958-
    The Stranger's Message / Paul McCusker.
        p.   cm.—(Adventures in Odyssey; 11)
    Summary: A homeless man's arrival in Odyssey challenges Whit and
the young people of the community to consider what it means to live
as Christians in difficult situations.
    ISBN 1-56179-537-2
    [1. Christian life—Fiction. 2. Honesty—Fiction.] I. Title.
II. Series: McCusker, Paul, 1958- Adventures in Odyssey; 11.
PZ7.M47841635Suf   1997
[Fic]--DC21   96-54640
                                                             CIP
                                                             AC

Published by Focus on the Family Publishing, Colorado Springs, CO 80995.

The author is represented by the literary agency of Alive Communications,
1465 Kelly Johnson Blvd., Suite 320, Colorado Springs, CO 80920.

This is a work of fiction, and any resemblance between the characters in this
book and real persons is coincidental.

Editor: Larry K. Weeden
Front cover illustration: JoAnn Weistling

Printed in the United States of America

97 98 99 00/10 9 8 7 6 5 4 3 2

Adventures in Odyssey Novel 11:
The Stranger's Message

Note: In 1897, Charles Sheldon wondered what would happen if an entire town decided to "do as Jesus would do" in their homes and workplaces. The answer was the classic novel *In His Steps*. It is this author's hope that our *Odysseyized* adaptation of the same concept will inspire readers to go back to the original book and take to heart its simple yet powerful message.

CHAPTER ONE

L ord, help me," John Avery Whittaker said under his breath as he sat down once again at the oak desk in his study. His plea for help had an uncharacteristic edge to it. He had been trying to assemble the questions for a Bible contest he was hosting at his shop, Whit's End, later that evening, but one interruption after another had conspired to keep him from his work. Three phone calls, a door-to-door salesman, the mail carrier, and a pesky fly that kept dive-bombing his nose had pushed the normally affable man to the limits of his patience.

He glanced around his study suspiciously, wondering what would interrupt him next. Maybe one of the many book-shelves would suddenly collapse, the window shade would violently flap upward, or a leg on the desk chair would break. It felt to him as if the very silence of the room might scream, if only to ruin his concentration. He stroked his bushy, white mustache and waited. Nothing happened.

Satisfied that he could go back to work, Whit (as he was best known) opened his Bible to find a verse in the book of James. He accidentally opened a couple of pages past it and found himself looking at a passage in the first letter of Peter, chapter two, verse 21. It said simply:

> To this you were called, because Ch.
> suffered for you, leaving you an exam₁
> that you should follow in his steps.

He stared at the verse with an unexplainable feeling that the words were significant. After a moment, he dismissed the feeling and then turned to the book of James.

The doorbell rang.

"I knew it," Whit groaned. He sat still as if afraid that if he moved, the bell might ring again. He secretly hoped whoever it was would go away. The doorbell rang again. Whit sighed, stood up, and gently moved the curtain aside on a window that gave him a clear view of the front porch.

A man stood on the steps, dressed in worn, dirty clothing. He had greasy, matted hair that looked as if it hadn't been washed or combed in a long time. Frowning at the work yet to be done on his desk, Whit went down the stairs to the door. It was the last straw—the last interruption he would tolerate—and he yanked the door open as if to warn whoever it was that he wasn't in a mood to be trifled with.

The stranger looked at Whit with a startled expression, as if he didn't expect anyone to answer the door. Whit gazed at him, not sure what to make of someone who looked so bad, then asked, "Can I help you?"

The stranger coughed nervously. "I'm out of work, sir, and thought you might know of someone who's hiring," he said. "Maybe to do some odd jobs . . ."

"I'm really sorry," Whit replied, "but I don't know of anything offhand. Try the shops downtown." He slowly began to close the door.

"Anything at all," the man said as he struggled to smile. "Just point me in the right direction." His teeth appeared yellow behind the gray stubble on his face. The lines around his eyes seemed to point like arrows at their redness.

Whit tried to imagine who he'd send a man in this condition to, but he couldn't think of anyone. "I wish I could help you," he said. "I really don't know of anyone who's hiring. And I don't have anything around here that needs to be done. I'm sorry. I hope you find something."

"Thanks anyway," the man said as he turned to leave.

Whit closed the door and went back up to his study. He was about to start working again but first yielded to the temptation to look out the window. The man had walked down the sidewalk to the street and now stood as if he couldn't decide which way to turn.

Whit let the curtain fall back into place. He felt a pang of guilt. He could have offered the man something temporary at Whit's End, he knew. There were floors to be swept, windows to be washed, dishes to be cleaned. Even around the house, Whit could have paid the man a few dollars to rake the leaves. A list formed in Whit's mind of all the things he could have done for the stranger but didn't think about at the time because he *had to* get the questions for the Bible contest finished.

It's not too late, Whit thought, and he leaped to his feet. He tossed aside the curtains and reached for the window, preparing to throw it open and call for the man to come back. His fingers were clasped around the latch when he saw the sidewalk and street were empty. The man was gone.

With a heavy heart, Whit sat down at his desk and slowly returned to the Bible contest questions. There were no other interruptions that afternoon.

****

Tom Riley, Whit's best friend, arrived as planned at 5:30 to pick Whit up for the evening's activities at Whit's End.

"Ready?" Tom asked in his gentle, folksy accent as Whit climbed into the passenger side of the car.

"I think so," Whit answered. "How did it go at the shop this afternoon?"

Tom pulled the car out of the driveway and into the street. "No particular problems," he said. "Except you might want to take a look at the train set. The Baltimore and Ohio keeps coming off the tracks. It won't be too long before they all come apart."

"I'll look at it later tonight," Whit said, knowing his friend was trying to make a point. *You need help,* Tom was really saying behind his comment about the train set. Whit knew it was true. Apart from sporting the county's largest running train, Whit's End also had an ice-cream parlor, a library, a theater, and dozens of rooms filled with interactive displays. It was little wonder that Whit's End had become one of the most popular places for the children in Odyssey to play. But the success of the shop made it hard for Whit to keep up with all the things needing to be taken care of, and harder still for him to find the right kind of people to work there.

Employees came and went quickly. Whit was never satisfied with any of their work. He figured he could do it all better himself. Tom had said just the other day that Whit was being "too picky." *Maybe he was right,* Whit thought. In all of Odyssey, Tom was the only one Whit trusted in the shop. Earlier in the afternoon, Tom had kept an eye on things while Whit worked on the Bible contest questions.

"You can't do it all," Tom said. "And I can't keep helping you. I have a farm to run."

"I know, Tom, and I'm grateful." Whit watched the sunset explode blues, yellows, and oranges behind the houses and, in the distance, the larger buildings of downtown Odyssey. They were approaching the edge of McAlister Park, where the autumn leaves spread like a carpet over the playing fields and under large collections of trees. Tom would have to drive around the edge of the park for another mile before reaching the Victorian-style building housing Whit's End.

Tom adjusted the shoulder strap on his overalls. "There was one peculiar thing that happened today," he said.

"Oh?" Whit's thick, white eyebrows lifted and nearly

blended with the wild, white hair on the top of his head.

Tom nodded. "A man I'd never seen before came in to Whit's End. He was a little shabby-looking, like he hadn't had a bath or changed his clothes in a long time."

Whit thought of the man who had come to his door that afternoon. "Did he say anything?"

"That's what was so odd. I thought he was going to ask for a handout, but he didn't. He just sat in one of the booths for a while and drank some water. He showed an interest in the posters for the Bible contest tonight, but he didn't say anything. After a while, he left."

Whit rubbed his chin thoughtfully and felt the pang of guilt again. He should have done something for the man. "Sounds like the same man who came to my door this afternoon. I'm ashamed to say I was so preoccupied with the Bible contest that I didn't offer to help him. I feel bad about it now."

Tom shook his head. "Funny you should mention it," he said. "I kept thinking that I should give the man some food, but I got so busy with the kids that I never did it. He was gone before I realized."

"So much for good intentions," Whit said.

They reached the front of Whit's End, where kids were already lined up to take part in the Bible contest. Whit grabbed his Bible and stack of questions from the front seat and didn't think again about the stranger—until later that evening when the stranger would be *all* he'd think about.

CHAPTER TWO

W hat did James say was like the small rudder of a ship?" Whit asked from his podium on the Little Theatre stage in Whit's End.

The remaining contestants, sitting in a semicircle, wiggled in their chairs and scratched their heads. Only five players remained. The rest had been eliminated throughout the evening by not knowing the answers to where specific Bible verses were found, who wrote what books, or which character did what and where he or she did it.

The Bible contest was one of the many methods Whit used to help bring the Bible to life for kids. He believed the more fun they had with Scripture, the more they'd get out of it. This evening's contest proved the point: The kids cheered and howled for the various contestants, calling out answers and groaning when an obvious answer escaped them. They didn't do it for the prize (which, in this case, was a week's worth of ice cream at Whit's End). They did it for the fun.

"The tongue!" Karen Crosby exclaimed in a burst of excitement and nearly fell out of her chair.

"You're right," Whit said. The crowd applauded as Whit turned over his question card. He picked up another. "Which three disciples went with Jesus to a high mountain where they saw Him speak with Elijah and Moses?"

Oscar's hand shot up. "Peter, John, and Matthew!" he shouted.

Whit smiled at the round-faced boy. "Sorry, Oscar. It wasn't," he said.

"Oh, man." Oscar frowned and gave up his seat on the stage. Whit was sorry to see the boy leave, since he was often teased for not being very bright. He had surprised everyone by making it so far into the contest.

"It was Peter, John, and *James!*" Lucy Cunningham-Schultz cried out in her mousy voice.

"You're correct!" Whit announced.

Lucy giggled, and Karen said graciously, "Good going, Lucy."

"All right, Lucy!" Jack Davis cheered from the audience. Then he and Matt Booker began to chant, "Looo-seee! Loooseee! Looo-seee!" until Whit waved his arms to quiet them down.

The field was narrowed to Lucy, Karen, Mike Henderson (a pastor's son), and Jamie Peck, a boy of 10 who was extremely smart for his age. Whit couldn't imagine who the winner would be since they were all so evenly matched.

He continued, "In the Gospel of Mark, chapter 10, a

young man asked Jesus what he must do to inherit eternal life. In verse 21, Jesus gave the young man specific instructions. What did He say to do?"

The contestants squirmed awkwardly as they each tried to think of the answer.

"Sell what you own and give the money to the poor, and follow Me," an adult male voice said from the back of the auditorium.

It was such a surprise that Whit almost said "Right!" before he realized the wrong person had spoken. Heads turned and necks craned to see who had answered. Whit shielded his eyes from the stage lights. He barely made out the form as it moved forward to the center of the audience.

"I'm sorry, but we don't allow answers from the audience," Whit said, still unable to see who had spoken.

"But that's the right answer," the man said. "Sell what you own and give the money to the poor, and follow Me."

The auditorium was ear-poppingly silent as the kids and some of the few attending parents watched with wide, worried eyes. Tom, who'd been standing in the wings, now took a few steps onto the stage to show that another adult was present—just in case the man meant to cause trouble.

The man walked closer to the stage, and Whit finally recognized him. It was the same man who had come to his door earlier in the afternoon. He was in the same drab, dirty clothes, with matted hair and scratchy stubble. Whit found nothing dangerous in the man's tone or in how he moved. In fact, Whit thought he looked like a man who might be walking and talking in his sleep. There was an unreal calm, even sadness, in his demeanor.

He rubbed a hand over his greasy hair and said, "I'm sorry to interrupt. I really am. But I was watching this contest—watching how good these kids are with their Bibles—and I thought I oughta say something. You see, I've been out of work for about 10 months. I was a printer in Connellsville, and the new computers took away my job. I don't have anything against computers or the folks who use them, but they put me out of work. What could I do? Printing is all I know—"

Whit held up a hand to interrupt. "Look, sir," he said, "maybe we should talk about this somewhere else."

The stranger shook his head. "Please," he said, "I won't take much of your time. I just thought you Bible-believing people might be interested in what I have to say. I'm not complaining. I was just sitting in the back, thinking that *knowing* about the Bible is one thing, while *doing* what the Bible says is another.

"You folks seem to have it all worked out about what Jesus said in the Bible, and that's a good thing. Even the young man in the chapter you read seemed to have it all worked out. He kept the Ten Commandments. But Jesus said to *follow* Him, and, well, the young man went away sad. I just wonder if we understand what it means when Jesus says to follow Him. Do we?"

Here the man slowly turned to look at his audience. The kids hung on every word. "What do we Christians mean by following in the steps of Jesus?

"I've been wandering around your town for two days, trying to find a job. I don't mean printing, I mean *any kind* of job. And in all that time, I haven't had a word of sympathy or comfort from anyone except your Mr. Whittaker here, who said he was sorry for me. Everyone else turned away—or turned me away.

"Now, I know you can't all go out of your way to find jobs for people like me. I'm not asking you to. I'm just trying to figure out how those words in the Bible connect to our real lives—to what we should say or do when someone in need comes up to us. When Jesus said to follow Him, *what did He mean?* Did He mean to just get on with our lives, or was He talking about something more—something that would make a difference in our world?"

He scanned the audience, then slowly continued, "I know what you're thinking. You're thinking I should be able to get a job somewhere if I really wanted one. That's what all the people who have jobs and homes and money say. They don't understand how hard it is. My wife died a few months ago, and I thank God she's out of this trouble. My daughter is . . . well, she's taken care of. I never wanted to be a burden to her or anybody else. But nobody in Connellsville could help me, so I made my way to Odyssey. I thought, *Here's a place where folks are living well. There's got to be something here for me.*"

The man stopped for a moment and pressed his hand against his mouth as if trying to stifle a scream. He swayed slightly. Whit and Tom took a step toward him but stopped when he spoke again.

"I'm puzzled, that's all. Everyone's doing so well in this town, and Jesus said things like 'Sell what you own, give money to the poor, and follow Me,' and I'm trying to figure it out in my mind. My wife died in a tenement building in Connellsville. It was owned by a Christian landlord, and even though she died, he told me I had to pay up my rent or leave right away. He was a Christian man and said he felt bad for making me leave. I guess he felt bad the same way the young man in the story felt bad.

"Jesus said to follow Him, and we always feel bad when we don't. Maybe we just don't understand what He means. Or maybe we do and we just feel bad because we don't think we can do what He wants. I don't know. Maybe we don't even ask ourselves what it really means to follow Him. Do we ever ask, 'What would Jesus do if He were in my situation?' What would Jesus do if He had a nice house and a good job and decent family but knew there were folks outside who didn't have any of those things? What would Jesus do to help folks like me who have to walk the streets or who die in tenements or who—"

The man suddenly cried out and jerked toward the stage as if someone had punched him from the side. He reached his hands out wildly, then fell to his knees. Spinning out of control, he grabbed the edge of the stage with a grimy hand for only a second before collapsing to the floor.

CHAPTER THREE

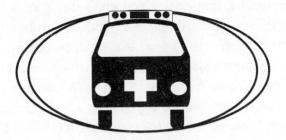

Whit rode to the hospital in the back of the ambulance with the unconscious stranger. A team of doctors and nurses met the gurney as it was brought into the emergency room. Whit started to follow as they wheeled it past a curtained area, but a doctor stopped him.

"Please wait out here," he said, pulling the curtains together. They rattled loudly across the rod.

Dazed by everything that had happened, Whit slowly paced back and forth in the lounge of the emergency area.

"I need some information about the patient," a nurse with a clipboard came out and told him a minute later. "Name?"

"I don't know," Whit said.

"Do you know *anything* about him?"

Whit shook his head. "Not really. He's a stranger. He collapsed in my shop."

"Then he isn't insured, is he?" the nurse asked.

"If you're worried about who'll pay," Whit replied, "I'll

take care of everything. Just help him, all right?"

The nurse handed Whit the clipboard. "Then I'll need you to fill this out and sign at the bottom."

Whit mechanically obeyed. Even as his fingers moved the pen through the little boxes asking for his name, address, and financial information, his mind raced with everything the stranger had said earlier. *Do I know what Jesus meant?* he asked himself again and again. *What does it really mean to follow Him? What does it mean to walk in His steps?*

The hands of the clock above the nurses' station moved indifferently past the hour—then past another hour. Whit sat staring at the torn, black leather on the waiting lounge sofa. The television was on, but the sound was off. Whit didn't pay attention to the fast-cutting images that flickered and flashed on the screen. *Does following Jesus mean just trying to be good, or does it mean something more? What does it mean to walk in His steps?*

"Well, Whit?"

Before he looked up, Whit recognized the voice. It was Captain Wilkins from the Odyssey police.

"Hi, Joe," Whit said.

Captain Wilkins sat down on a small chair nearby. He was dressed in casual clothes, as if he'd been called from an evening at home. His jacket was partially zipped up over a flannel shirt.

"Is it cold outside?" Whit asked. He had forgotten to bring his own coat.

"A typical fall night. Crisp," the captain replied. "Tom

told me what happened at Whit's End. I guess some of the kids and parents are still shook up. What can you tell me about the stranger?"

Whit sighed and said, "Not much. He said he was an unemployed printer in Connellsville. His wife died a few months ago in a tenement owned by a Christian. He has a daughter, but he didn't say where she was. That's all."

"It's a start," Wilkins said. "He didn't have a wallet or any identification. I can check with the printers' union, though. And the Connellsville police may be able to help me with tracking down information about the dead wife."

Whit glanced at the captain. His words sounded so cold and clinical, as if the stranger were an abandoned car instead of a human being.

Captain Wilkins leaned toward Whit. "They told me you're going to take care of his bills. Why? You've never seen him before today, right?"

"He came to my door this afternoon and the shop tonight."

"You don't have to feel obligated, Whit," Wilkins said. "He's not your responsibility."

"Isn't he?" Whit asked.

Dr. Morton appeared in the doorway of the waiting lounge. Her white coat was rumpled, and her hands were shoved deep in its pockets. She looked tired. "Whit?" she said.

Whit looked up at her.

"Your friend has a damaged heart," she said. "There isn't much we can do. Right now he's in a coma."

****

The doctors moved the stranger to the intensive care ward. Since no one had been able to find any information about the next of kin, Dr. Morton gave permission for Whit to sit with him. Apart from a patient in a bed across the floor, all the other beds were empty. The stranger was attached to all kinds of tubes and equipment. A heart monitor blipped a green line on a black screen. Its effect on Whit was hypnotic. Up and down, up and down the line went.

It was close to ten o'clock when one of the nurses signaled Whit to come out into the hall. Tom Riley was waiting for him, clutching a coat in his hands.

"How's our mystery man?" Tom asked.

"In a coma," Whit answered, then moved to the vending machine to get a cup of coffee. He slid the coins into the slot and watched as the cup dropped and slowly filled with the dark-brown liquid. "He has a bad heart."

Tom shook his head. "That's too bad. Are you planning to spend the night here?"

"I think I should. Don't you?"

Tom shrugged. "I can stay with him for a while if you get tired."

"Thanks."

The two men looked at each other with a deep understanding. They were both affected by the stranger and all he had said. His words hadn't been idle or the ramblings of a lunatic. He had spoken calmly and asked them a simple question that cut to the very heart of their Christianity. The Bible spoke of entertaining angels unaware. Whit and Tom took the notion seriously. And even if the stranger wasn't an angel, his words seemed to come from heavenly places.

"We canceled the contest," Tom said. "I used the rest of the time to talk to the kids and their parents. Some were pretty upset. I guess we were all just trying to figure out what to make of what he said."

"Did any of you come to a conclusion?" Whit picked up the cup of coffee and blew the steam across the top.

"No. There wasn't much to say—everyone felt bad—we all wished we had done more to help him." Tom shuffled uneasily. "I think most of us got to wondering about his question. You know, what does it mean to follow Jesus?"

"Me, too."

They stood in silence again. The hospital hallway was empty.

"Let's pray, Tom."

Tom agreed, and the two men bowed their heads then and there. They didn't say much out loud except to ask God to heal the stranger and help them understand the meaning behind the evening's events.

When they finished, Tom held up the coat in his hand. It was plain brown, torn, and grease-smeared. "I found this in the back of the auditorium," he said. "I think it's his."

Whit took it. "Thanks for everything, Tom."

"Oh, and I brought your car. Third row back from the front entrance." Tom handed him the extra set of keys Whit kept at the shop for emergencies. "I'll get a lift back from Donnie Armstrong. He's an orderly downstairs. His shift is about to end. Good kid. Used to be in my Sunday school class."

Whit nodded. He remembered Donnie.

"You call me if you want me to come back. I mean it. I'll stay."

"I will." Whit watched his friend walk down the hallway with a renewed feeling of gratitude.

Back in the intensive care ward, the stranger remained unconscious. Whit sat down with his coffee and realized that the stranger's coat might have some identification in the pockets. He checked the outside ones first, discovering only a fragment of an old sandwich and some plastic-wrapped saltine crackers. His fingers felt the inside breast pocket and made contact with a small paper bag that had been carefully folded down to a rectangle. Whit opened the bag: It held three letters. Each one was addressed to Raymond Clark. In the upper-left-hand corner, above an address in Columbus, Ohio, was the name of Christine Holt.

Whit slipped out of the room to phone Captain Wilkins.

****

"Raymond Clark of Connellsville," Captain Wilkins confirmed an hour later over the phone. "His wife's name was Mary. Christine Holt is his daughter. Holt is her married name. We've been trying to reach her in Columbus, but we haven't had much success. I think the Columbus police are going to send someone around to the address you gave me. I'll let you know if we learn any more."

"Joe," Whit said slowly, his speech a little slurred from his weariness, "if it's a matter of money . . . I mean, if his daughter needs help to get here . . . leave it to me."

"If you say so," Wilkins said. They hung up. Whit was aware of a surge of activity down the hall—in the intensive care ward—and felt a sick feeling go through his stomach. He walked quickly and then found himself running back to Raymond Clark's bed. Two nurses were at its side, adjusting equipment and checking his vital signs.

"Promise me," Raymond Clark was saying when Whit arrived.

"He's talking?" Whit asked, surprised.

"Stay back, Mr. Whittaker," one of the nurses said.

"Promise me," Raymond Clark said again. His voice was a harsh whisper.

Whit got as close to the bed as he could without getting in the nurses' way.

"Promise you what?" Whit asked gently. "Mr. Clark?"

Raymond Clark turned his head slightly. His eyes were red and wet, but he fixed them on Whit. "You're a kind man. My daughter. Promise me you'll tell her where I am."

"I promise," Whit said. "In fact, we found her letters in your coat pocket. We're going to bring her to see you as fast as we can."

"She won't . . ." His voice trailed off to a mumble, then returned with, ". . . in time. I know. I'm not afraid. Do you see Him? Jesus is . . ."

Raymond Clark slowly closed his eyes. The green line on the heart monitor machine stopped bouncing and went flat across the screen. The room was filled with the sound of a solitary, unending beep.

The nurses and doctors were powerless to save his life.

****

"Go home and get some sleep," Dr. Morton advised Whit later in the waiting lounge. "There's nothing you can do."

Whit rubbed his eyes. They burned from lack of sleep and the tears that wouldn't fall. *Nothing you can do*, Whit thought again and again as he drove home. In a few hours, another Sunday morning would arrive in Odyssey. People would get up and go to church as they always did, unaware of—or uncaring about—the Raymond Clarks in the world who had slept hungry the night before . . . or died.

Nothing you can do, Dr. Morton had said.

Whit braked his car to a halt in his driveway and leaned against the steering wheel. *Well,* he thought, *we'll just see about that.*

CHAPTER FOUR

Lucy walked into the sanctuary of Odyssey Community Church and scanned the half-filled pews. It was still early. Most of the congregation hadn't yet wandered in from their various Sunday school classes. Lucy clutched her Bible and noticed smudges of white powder on the cover. She smiled to herself. It was baby powder from changing David Kemper's diaper in the nursery.

Karen Crosby waved from her normal spot on the pew on the side of the church. She was sitting with Jack, Matt, and Oscar—*the Three Musketeers*, Lucy called them, because they'd been together so much lately. Lucy strolled over and slid in next to the gang.

"Where've you been?" Karen asked. "You weren't in Sunday school."

Lucy held out her white fingers and said, "Nursery."

"Something's going on," Matt said.

"What do you mean?" Lucy asked.

Jack leaned forward. "Mr. Whittaker wasn't in Sunday school. Mrs. Winger covered for him."

Oscar chimed in, "When we asked if he was sick, she said no and not to ask any questions because we'd find out in church. Isn't that weird? Mr. Whittaker *never* misses teaching his class."

"I think it has something to do with the man," Karen said.

"The one who barged in on the contest last night," Jack clarified, as if Lucy had already forgotten the incident.

Oscar looked around nervously, then said, "I heard he was a lunatic and they took him away to the asylum."

"I heard he was once the pastor of *this* church and came back because they fired him," Jack said.

"Cut it out," Lucy said. "You guys don't know what you're talking about."

"But something happened," Karen affirmed.

Mr. Shelton started playing a hymn on the organ as a signal for all talking to stop. The sanctuary slowly filled up with the regular church attendees and a few people Lucy didn't recognize. During the first hymn, Pastor Henderson walked up to his chair behind the pulpit. Whit followed and sat down in the guest chair next to it.

"See? I told you," Jack said, gesturing to Whit.

Whit looked tired, as if he'd been sick or up all night. Lucy tried to take in the eyes beneath the wild, white hair. They were puffy. And his normal smiling expression seemed undone by a sad droop in his mustache.

The church service proceeded as usual, with hymns,

Scripture readings, announcements, and the offering. After the collection plates had been passed by, then removed, another hymn was sung as a lead-in to the pastor's sermon. The hymn was "Take My Life and Let It Be."

As the last note of the hymn echoed through the church, Pastor Henderson stepped up to the pulpit. He spoke in a tone so serious that Lucy instinctively drew her arms around herself. "Good morning, ladies and gentlemen," he said. "Thank you for joining us. I'm sure by now most of you have heard about what happened at Whit's End last night. But just in case you haven't, allow me a minute to explain."

He went on to tell the congregation about the Bible contest at Whit's End, how it had been interrupted by the stranger, what he had said before he collapsed, and how he had been taken to the hospital, where he later died.

Lucy put her hand over her mouth as she gasped along with others in the congregation. She didn't know what she had expected to hear about the stranger, but she had never thought he was going to die.

The pastor continued, "John Whittaker, who was with the stranger until the end, has asked to talk to the church this morning. After hearing what he wants to say, I believe it's the best thing for all of us. Please give him your full attention. Whit?"

"Thank you, Pastor Henderson," Whit said when he reached the pulpit. He spoke so softly that Lucy had to strain her ears to hear him. "I'm grateful to those of you who were at Whit's End last night—and to those of you who prayed for

Raymond Clark. That was his name. We still don't have all the details about him, but I understand he has a daughter who is being notified."

Whit clutched the pulpit as if it were the only thing stopping him from falling over. Lucy felt an unfamiliar tightness in her chest.

Surveying the audience, Whit continued, "The appearance of Mr. Clark at Whit's End last night startled us all. It's not often we have a complete stranger come in, looking like he did and talking the way he talked. But I have to tell you honestly: His words hit me right here"—Whit put his hand over his heart. "And when I think that those were the last words he spoke in public before he died, they hit me even harder.

"Do you know what he asked us? He wanted to know what it means when we say we're followers of Jesus. What difference does it make to our lives? Ask anyone who heard him. He wasn't harsh or judgmental. He simply asked the question, then pointed out how different following Jesus is from how we normally live our lives. I wish I could ignore Mr. Clark and his words—it'd be easier that way—but I can't. What he said was true. What he asked was something we should all be asking ourselves every day of our lives. What does it mean to follow Jesus? What would change in my life if I truly walked in His steps?"

Whit paused again. The congregation shuffled uncomfortably. Someone coughed. Lucy braced herself—for what, she didn't know. But all her instincts said that this was serious—*very* serious.

"I have a plan in mind," Whit said. "Call it a challenge, if you want. But I've been thinking about Mr. Clark's question and how to answer him. What I propose now is something that shouldn't be peculiar to any of us, but it will probably sound ridiculous, even impossible. Basically, I'm looking for volunteers to pledge themselves—for just a couple of weeks—to do only what Jesus would do."

The congregation came alive with buzzing and whispers.

Whit held up his hand for silence so he could continue. "The idea is for us not to do anything without first asking the question, *What would Jesus do?* And afterward, we ought to act as we believe Jesus Himself would act if He were in our place. I'm pledging myself to that challenge right here and now. I'm asking for others to join me—men and women, boys and girls. Make no mistake. It's a simple challenge, but it won't be easy. But I'm willing to try. If you are, too, meet me at Whit's End this afternoon at 3:00. That's all I have to say."

Whit stepped away from the pulpit, and Pastor Henderson returned to close the service in prayer. After the final hymn, the entire auditorium exploded in conversation.

Lucy wondered if she should take Whit up on his challenge. *What would Jesus do?* she asked herself.

CHAPTER FIVE

H e didn't get many people to show up," Jack observed from the booth in the far corner of the Whit's End soda shop. He was there with Lucy, Karen, Matt, and Oscar. They had all agreed after church to go to the meeting. Lucy and Karen were serious about taking Whit up on his challenge. Jack, Matt, and Oscar just wanted to see what would happen next.

"I count 16 adults," Oscar said. "So counting us that would be . . ."

"Twenty-one," Matt finished for him with a bored tone in his voice.

Lucy adjusted her glasses and scanned the room to see who had shown up. Most of them were leaders from the church, including Pastor Henderson and Tom Riley, who was a deacon. The others were parents (including Lucy's and Karen's parents and Oscar's mom).

"They're the ones I figured would come," Jack said.

Matt nodded. "They *had* to show up—or they'd look like they weren't spiritual," he said.

"Maybe they thought it was a good idea," Karen said, annoyed at Jack's and Matt's sarcastic attitudes. She slumped over the table and weaved a finger through her chestnut hair as she always did when she was bothered about something.

Whit stood up in front of the small gathering. "Thank you for coming," he said. He looked pale and even more tired than he had just a few hours before. Lucy thought he was on the verge of tears. "Let's pray."

All heads were bowed. From Whit's very first words— "Dear Father"—something about the room seemed to change. Lucy felt it so precisely that she glanced up as if someone had tapped her on the shoulder. She caught eyes with Karen, who was also looking around with a confused expression. Oscar furrowed his brow while Jack and Matt, eyes still closed, wiggled in their seats. Out of the corner of her eye, Lucy saw the adults in the room also reacting to whatever it was that seemed to be happening because of Whit's prayer. The hair stood up on the back of her neck— but not from fear, from *excitement*. It was as if the room were suddenly charged with electricity.

"The Holy Spirit," Karen whispered.

Lucy bowed her head and knew He was there. She felt it as surely as she felt the presence of the rest of the kids at her table. And somehow she knew this wasn't just an experiment or a game. Whit's challenge was *real*—and not to be taken lightly. But she knew she *would* take the challenge. She *would* try to follow in the steps of Jesus in what she did over the next couple of weeks. The presence of the Spirit—if that's what it really was—confirmed in her heart that she *had to*.

When Whit finished his prayer, everyone sat silently, heads still bowed, as if hesitant to interrupt whatever they were feeling.

Whit's face was wet with tears. He pulled a handkerchief from his pocket and wiped his eyes. "I hope we understand what we're here to do," he said. "Basically, we're here to pledge to ask what Jesus would do with *everything* in our lives. Then we'll act on the answer we get, regardless of the consequences. Do we all agree?"

Karen suddenly raised her hand and said, "Excuse me, Mr. Whittaker. I have a question."

"Go ahead, Karen."

She cleared her throat shyly, then said, "Well, I want to do what Jesus would do. But I'm not really sure I *know* what He would do. I don't remember any stories in the Bible about Jesus taking a math class or learning to play volleyball in gym class."

A few scattered chuckles echoed around the room. Whit smiled. "That's a very good question, Karen," he assured her. "My guess is that all of us will have to consider carefully how Jesus would act in our homes or schools or offices. It's a different world now from the one He lived in, yet His truth is timeless. The only thing we can do is study Jesus in Scripture and rely on the Holy Spirit to guide us. There are no easy rules for how to do it. We just have to read our Bibles, pray, and talk to people who are wiser than we are."

"But what if someone disagrees and says Jesus wouldn't do what we think He'd do?" Pastor Henderson asked.

Whit shrugged. "That'll probably happen. I don't expect everyone to agree with what we're trying to do or how we do it. There'll be some struggles to get it right. We just have to be completely honest and open with ourselves about our decisions. If someone says we're wrong, we'll have to prayerfully consider their opinion and test it to see if the Spirit is speaking through them. But in the long run, I think there'll be consistency in our decision making. If we're in tune with the Holy Spirit, there shouldn't be any confusion in how we decide. But we have to be committed once we've made our decision. Right?"

The adults nodded their agreement. Then someone else asked another question that led to a long, grown-up conversation that didn't interest the kids in the corner booth very much.

Lucy turned to Jack and Matt. "Are you going to do it?" she asked.

"Are you?" Matt said.

Lucy said yes.

"If it's good enough for you, it's good enough for us," Jack said, then nudged Oscar. "Right?"

"Right," Oscar said.

"It's not a competition," said Lucy.

Jack rolled his eyes. "I know," he said as if stating the obvious.

But Lucy suspected deep inside that he *didn't* know.

"Look, it's not like it's going to be so hard," Matt said. "I mean, it's not as if we have anything really serious to deal with. For me, it'll be trying to figure out what Jesus would do with my next English assignment."

"I think there's more to it than that," Karen said. "It's going to affect *everything* in our lives. I'm the president of the student council. What would Jesus do with our student council?"

"Tell them all to resign," Jack said with a laugh.

Lucy frowned. "Oh boy. I'm the editor of the *Odyssey Owl*. How would Jesus edit a school newspaper?"

Lucy and Karen exchanged uneasy glances.

"We don't have anything to worry about," Matt said. "Do we?"

Oscar didn't look convinced. He was chewing the inside of his mouth the way he did when he was trying to think.

"What's wrong, Oscar?" Jack asked.

"Well," Oscar said carefully, "I was just trying to figure out what Jesus would do when Joe Devlin and his gang try to beat me up after school."

"Turn the other cheek?" Karen asked.

"That's what I *always* do," Oscar said. "It doesn't help."

Whit was suddenly standing next to the booth, and Lucy realized the meeting had broken up and the adults were leaving. "I don't know if doing what Jesus would do will always *help* things," Whit said. "At least, not in the ways we expect. It's not like a magic formula to take our problems away or make us successful. Following Jesus is just . . . well, walking where He leads us. The question is, are we all committed to following Him wherever He goes?"

Whit's gaze fell from one face to another.

"Yes," Lucy said.

"Uh huh," Matt said.

Jack nodded. "Yep."

"Yes, sir," Oscar piped up.

"Me, too," Karen said. Then she sighed, curling a strand of hair around her finger. "I hope we know what we're getting ourselves into."

CHAPTER SIX

The next morning, Lucy slipped into the room that served as the main office for the *Odyssey Owl*. The bell wouldn't ring for school to start for another 15 minutes. She sat down next to a large, rectangular table covered with finished articles, assignment sheets, and clip-art catalogs. The silence of the room filled her with peace. She had determined to start the day the way Jesus often started His: with prayer. *I'm going to need it*, she figured.

She folded her hands and bowed her head, but it didn't feel right. She scooted the chair back, slid off, and knelt with her elbows on the edge of the seat. Her heart pounded a little harder as she whispered, "Dear God . . ."

She'd only been praying for a minute when Mike Colman, one of the *Owl's* reporters, walked in. Embarrassed, Lucy leaped to her feet.

"What's wrong?" Mike asked as he tossed his books on the table.

"Nothing," Lucy answered. "You startled me."

Mike cocked an eyebrow at her, then peered at the base of the table. "What were you doing down there? Did you drop something?"

"Never mind," Lucy said. "What are you doing here?"

Mike looked at her suspiciously. "It's Monday, right? Assignments for this week's issue?"

Lucy blushed. "Oh yeah." She fumbled for the assignment sheet that she'd worked out last Friday. "Let's see . . ."

"I was thinking I'd like to do something different this week," Mike said.

Lucy looked up at him.

"I want to do a movie review. I saw Sylvester Kostenagger's latest over the weekend. *Blood Runs Deep*. It was amazing."

"But that's an adult movie," Lucy said. "I heard it's nothing but violence and killing from beginning to end."

Mike put his hands on his hips. "You heard wrong. They stop blowing people away long enough to do a love scene in the middle."

"You're kidding."

"Nope." Mike smiled at her. His perfect white teeth, dimples, and curly, black hair reminded Lucy she once had a crush on him. "All the kids are talking about this movie. We have to review it. Besides, I got to interview Sylvester Kostenagger on the phone."

"What?"

Mike said proudly, "My dad's lawyer's brother-in-law is

an agent in Sylvester's talent agency, and he set it up for me to interview him. We talked for a whole five minutes. I even recorded it. I could do a review of the movie *and* print the interview!"

Lucy was instantly excited for Mike. What a scoop! And it was true that all the kids in the school had been looking forward to this new action thriller. Most of the kids' parents would take them to see it—or they'd sneak in as Mike probably had. The theater owners didn't seem to care as long as they got their money. But to have an interview with the actor himself—that's the kind of thing that could get the *Owl* mentioned in the *Odyssey Times!*

Lucy nearly said "Okay," but she stopped herself just before the word came out. What happened to the pledge she had made? "I'm going to have to think about it," she finally said.

"Think about it?" Mike was aghast. "What's to think about?"

She didn't dare tell him that she first had to decide what Jesus would do. Would Jesus, if He were editor of the *Owl,* allow a review to be printed about a movie that blatantly glorified violence?

Of course He wouldn't, Lucy knew. She then asked herself *how* she knew it. And in an instant, her mind worked through her reasons. For one thing, Jesus said to love each other—our neighbors, even our enemies. There was no room for that kind of love in movies where people got shot and buildings were blown up just for the fun of it. Lucy also remembered her parents' complaining about how violent movies made people less than human—they were just nameless and faceless characters who died—and Jesus certainly wouldn't approve of that. There was never a point to those violent movies, except to show more and more violence. They never taught the kinds of things Jesus taught about: mercy, compassion, self-sacrifice. There were more reasons, but Lucy figured she had enough.

"No," she said to Mike. "No review."

Mike was clearly disappointed, even shocked, but he rallied. "We'll just do the interview then," he suggested.

"Huh uh," she said and braced herself for the explosion.

"Are you nuts?" Mike shouted. "I talked to *Sylvester* on the phone! He answered my questions! He even said he'd send me an autographed picture!"

"No, Mike."

"Why not?" he demanded.

"Because movies like *Blood Runs Dark*—"

"Deep," he corrected her. "*Blood Runs Deep.*"

"Movies like that aren't healthy for kids like us. They're probably not healthy for adults, either. And actors like Sylvester what's-his-name don't even care what kind of effect their movies have on us. They're just out to make money."

"So what?"

"So there's nothing that says I have to promote his movie by printing a review or promote *him* by printing an interview."

Mike stared at her with his mouth hanging open. He looked as if he might rush into the hall and call for the school nurse to help poor Lucy, who'd finally flipped her wig. "This is a joke, right?" he said. "You're pulling my leg."

"No, I'm not."

"Then you've gone out of your mind!" he cried. "How could you *not* print a review, *especially* when I have an interview with the country's *biggest movie star* to go with it? What kind of editor are you, anyway?"

Lucy weighed her options carefully. There was a time when Mike and his family went to her church. They stopped going a couple of years ago and, for all she knew, had started going somewhere else. But one thing was certain: She had to tell him the real reason she couldn't print his review and interview.

"Close the door," she said softly.

He looked at her, puzzled, then obeyed.

Once the door was closed and he returned to face her, she explained, "Mike, the truth is, I can't print your stuff because . . . well, it isn't something that Jesus would do."

He stared at her for a moment, then blinked a couple of times as if he hadn't heard right. "Jesus? You mean, like, Jesus in the Bible?"

Lucy nodded. "I made a pledge yesterday to do everything the way I think Jesus would do things. That includes my being the editor of the *Owl*. I don't think Jesus would print your review or interview. Do you?"

"No, He probably wouldn't." Then Mike shook his head quickly. "But . . . but this is crazy. You can't edit a paper like Jesus would. He never even edited a paper, did He? If He did, do you think any of the kids in this school would read it? I wouldn't."

"That's not the point. I made a pledge—no matter what," Lucy said.

"It's nuts," Mike said. "You'll get yourself in big trouble."

Lucy shrugged. "It's a risk I'll have to take."

****

At lunch, Lucy found Karen in the cafeteria, praying over her meal. Lucy had never seen Karen—or anyone, for that matter—pray over a school lunch. Lucy followed her lead when she sat down with her own sack lunch.

"Well?" Lucy asked after she said amen.

"Well what?" Karen said before chomping down on a fish stick.

"How's it going on the first day of your pledge?"

"Okay, I guess," Karen replied. "I nearly got in an argument with Donna Barclay about borrowing my brush, but I realized it wasn't something Jesus would argue about. Didn't He say something about giving away your coat if someone asked?"

Lucy nodded. "And to walk an extra mile."

"Yeah. So I gave Donna my brush." Karen pushed a lock of her hair away from her plate. "I have to meet this afternoon with Mr. Laker to talk about the stationery for the student council. Big deal."

"The student council is getting its own stationery? Why?"

"To write down all the high-powered decisions we're going to make," Karen said sarcastically. "I voted against the idea. I thought we could use the money to do more-important things. But I was in the minority, and it's my job to pick what it'll look like. How about you? How's the pledge going?"

"I'm not sure." Lucy bit into her ham sandwich. "I think everything's all right."

Karen looked at her skeptically. "That's not what I heard. Mike's been telling everyone you dumped his review and interview because you're on some wacko religious kick."

"Oh, no!" Lucy groaned.

"I couldn't believe you did it," Karen said proudly. "That must've been hard for you."

Lucy shook her head. "It wasn't as hard as I thought it would be. Once I figured out *why* Jesus would have said no to the movie review and interview, I knew I had a good case against it. But maybe that's the trick here: *Doing* the right thing might start off easy, but living with the outcome may be the tough part."

"Mike says he's going to complain to Mrs. Stegner," Karen said. Mrs. Stegner was an English teacher and the faculty sponsor of the *Odyssey Owl*. Ultimately, she was responsible for everything to do with the newspaper. "Do you think she'll back you up?"

"I guess I'll find out when she calls me in."

"What if she doesn't?"

"Then I'll have to decide what Jesus would do next."

****

Mr. Art Laker was the school administrator, in charge of the school's money. He made sure the textbooks were ordered, the teachers had enough chalk and erasers, and the secretary had all the paper clips she needed. He was a tall, heavyset man with a shiny, bald head, small eyes, and a face that went beet red whenever he got agitated. Karen always felt uncomfortable around him for no other reason than the feeling that he didn't really like his job. She had heard the other day that he was going to retire at the end of the school year. *He probably can't wait*, Karen thought as she walked into the school office.

Mrs. Stewart smiled as Karen stepped up to the office counter. "Hi, Karen," she said.

"Hi. I'm here to see Mr. Laker," Karen responded.

Mrs. Stewart looked puzzled. "Oh?" she said. "Well, I'm sorry, but he had an unexpected meeting at the district office. What were you meeting him about? Maybe I can help."

"I have to pick out the stationery design for the student council," Karen explained.

Mrs. Stewart chuckled and said, "Ah, the president is making big executive decisions, huh?"

"Yeah," Karen answered with a grin. "Our lives will never be the same once we have this stationery."

Gesturing to the small door leading behind the counter, Mrs. Stewart said, "Come on back to his office. He was looking at designs this morning, probably to get ready for your meeting together."

They walked back to Mr. Laker's closet-sized office down the corridor from the other, more important offices. Karen suspected that Mr. Laker probably resented being stuck down the hall in a tiny office when Principal Felegy and Vice Principal Santini had offices that were so much bigger and nicer looking. Even the school nurse had a bigger work area.

"There it is," Mrs. Stewart said, pointing to the stationery book spread across Mr. Laker's plain metal desk. "Have a seat and pick out what you want."

Karen sat down at the desk to look through the various designs. The catalog had all types and sizes. Some of the lettering was boxy-looking, some had curlycues, some looked too boyish, and others were too girlish. Choosing one wasn't going to be easy. Ten minutes later, after her eyes started to hurt, she found the one she liked best: an austere "Times New Roman" type set at 14 points. She scribbled down what she thought the letterhead should say: "From Your Student Council." She figured that phrase would encompass everything they needed to communicate with both the faculty and students.

"It looks like it has strength and authority," Mrs. Stewart said when she saw Karen's choice.

"Yeah, I guess," Karen said with a shrug. It was hard for her to take the job very seriously. "Now we have to get bids."

"Bids?"

"You know—I have to ask some printing companies how much it'll cost to make the stationery, then go with the cheapest."

Mrs. Stewart rolled her eyes. "I know what *bids* are, but you don't have to go to all that trouble. We have a company that'll do all the printing for you."

Karen frowned. "But Mr. Felegy told me at the beginning of the year that we always had to get bids on *everything* we do. He said it was county school board policy or something like that."

"Mr. Laker has one company he always works with," Mrs. Stewart explained patiently.

Karen felt confused about the contradiction between what Mr. Felegy had said and what Mr. Laker did, but she honestly didn't care enough to argue. "What's their phone number?" she asked.

Mrs. Stewart pulled open a drawer on a tall, gray filing cabinet. She thumbed through some of the manila folders. "It *should* be here," she said. She looked around the office, then spied something in an open briefcase. After a quick look, she grabbed it up. "Here it is. Ballistic Printing," she said.

"Funny name."

Laura Szypulski, a student assistant in the office, appeared in the doorway and breathlessly said, "Mrs. Stewart! Mr. Felegy wants you in the gym right away! Somebody fell off the balance beam and got knocked out!"

"Oh!" Mrs. Stewart cried out. She tossed the file into Karen's lap. "Take it," she said, then waved wildly for her to get out. "Students aren't allowed in here unsupervised. I have to lock everything up."

"But the file—"

"Just bring it back later."

Karen obeyed, clutching the file while Mrs. Stewart and Laura ushered her out, locked the main door to the office, and scurried down the hall toward the gym.

****

"What's this all about, Lucy?" Mrs. Stegner asked. They were sitting in the *Owl's* so-called office. Lucy had been asked to stop in before going on to her last class of the day. "Mike makes it sound like you've joined some kind of cult. I half expected you to walk in with your head shaved."

Lucy giggled. "No, ma'am," she said, trying to sound serious.

"Then what's going on? Why did you refuse to print Mike's review and interview?"

Lucy took a deep breath, then tried to explain her reasons without mentioning her pledge to do what Jesus would do. Mrs. Stegner nodded quietly as Lucy spoke.

"I understand," she said when Lucy finished her list of reasons.

Lucy was relieved. "Do you?"

"Yes, your reasons are sound," Mrs. Stegner said. "But what confuses me is why you're taking this position *now*. We've printed reviews of movies that were far more questionable than this one by Sylvester whoever-he-is. Why are you making an issue of it now?"

Lucy looked Mrs. Stegner in the eye and said with conviction, "Because I made a pledge to do what Jesus would do, and I don't think He'd support that movie."

"Ah, I see," Mrs. Stegner said as she leaned back in her chair. "You're trying to act as Jesus would act. That certainly explains the rumors."

"I don't know why everyone has to make a fuss about it," Lucy said.

Mrs. Stegner smiled. "They're making a fuss because it's a rather . . . er, *different* idea. By deciding not to print Mike's material, you're taking a moral stand that you haven't taken before. That's going to stir up some people. Not everyone thinks it's the editor's job to bring his or her personal morality into the newsroom. Some might say you're shoving your beliefs down other people's throats."

"Am I?" Lucy asked sincerely. She didn't want to argue, but she felt it was worth defending her position. "I mean, if I went ahead and printed Mike's stuff, I'd be making another moral decision, right? I'd be saying that Sylvester Kostenwhatsit's movies are okay and that kids should go see them. Why does it only seem 'moral' when you hold something back?"

"Good question," Mrs. Stegner said.

Lucy felt flushed now, but continued: "And since when does a person have to split up what they believe personally from what they do at school, or in an office, or at a newspaper? Didn't you just teach last week that most of our newspapers were started by people who *always* brought their personal perspectives to what they printed? They still do, except they never admit it now. Didn't you say so?"

"As a matter of fact, I *did* say that, but—"

"Then why can't I do that with the *Owl?*"

Mrs. Stegner laughed. "You're a sharp girl, Lucy. I respect what you think—you're sensible and show good judgment. That's why I asked you to be this year's editor. I'm not saying I disapprove of what you're trying to do. In fact, I'm very curious about it, as a sort of experiment."

"Really?"

Mrs. Stegner sat up in her chair and leaned forward on the table. "I assume you have other ideas for the newspaper. Surely we're doing a lot of things that Jesus wouldn't approve of."

"We sure are!" Lucy said excitedly. "I was thinking that we should get rid of that sarcastic tone we always seem to write in. Why can't we be more positive about our news?"

"Give me an example."

"Bruce Goff's column is one. He's always writing about how bad it is here at school, what a pain in the neck homework is, and how bad the cafeteria food is."

Mrs. Stegner picked up a pen and tapped it against her notepad. "Bruce probably speaks for most of the students," she suggested.

"He doesn't speak for anybody *I* know," Lucy said. "If things were as bad as Bruce says, we'd all be home schooled."

"That's just his particular perspective."

"Not just his perspective, but that of everybody who writes for the *Owl*. I know because I write that way myself. We're always talking about what's wrong. Why do we have to be so negative?" Lucy shook her head and continued, "I'm not afraid to report negative things that're really important, but I think they should be balanced by articles that show what's going *right* around here, too. I'd like to try it."

"It won't sell newspapers. It never does," Mrs. Stegner said.

"But if I'm going to keep my pledge, I have to try." Lucy paused for a moment, weighing carefully what she had to say next. "Mrs. Stegner, if this pledge doesn't work . . . I mean, if my decisions wreck the paper for some reason, I'll resign. I won't be editor anymore. Is that a deal?"

Mrs. Stegner gazed at Lucy soberly, then said, "Deal."

Lucy stood up to leave. "Thanks for being so understanding."

"Like I said, this is an interesting experiment," Mrs. Stegner said. "I sincerely hope it works."

****

Mr. Laker walked into the school office with his coat draped over his arm. Though it was overcast and crisply cool outside, he perspired. He waved at Mrs. Stewart as he walked past her desk.

"How was your meeting?" she asked.

He grunted. "The usual nonsense. Did I miss anything here?"

"Kevin Cassidy fell off the balance beam and hit his head. Three stitches."

"That's too bad," Mr. Laker said. He walked into his office. Mrs. Stewart followed. "We weren't at fault, were we?" he suddenly asked.

"Not that I know of. He was playing around."

"Oh." He stood behind his desk and looked down at the stationery catalog.

"Karen Crosby came in for her meeting with you."

"Meeting?"

She gestured to the catalog. "To choose the student council stationery. Remember?"

"Oh, that's right." He tossed his coat over the top of the filing cabinet.

"She picked a nice design, I think," Mrs. Stewart said.

"Good."

"She wanted to get bids for the job, but I told her we have a company we regularly work with." She put a finger to her chin as she remembered something. "Oh, I have to get that file back from her."

"File?" Mr. Laker asked as he sat down.

"For Ballistic Printing. In the panic that Kevin Cassidy caused, I gave her your file so she could call them."

Mr. Laker ran a hand over his bald scalp. "Why would *she* call them? That's for our office to do."

"Because she's the president of the student council, and

she's supposed to take responsibility for it. Practical experience, you see."

"I get it." He sat down as if to start working, then suddenly looked up at Mrs. Stewart. "Did you say you *gave* her my file? Which file? I took it with me to my meeting."

"No, you didn't. It was right there in your briefcase."

His face turned a slight pink. "You should never give my files to the students. Particularly files from my briefcase!"

"I'm sorry, I was—"

"What if she loses it? What if there's something confidential in it?" His face flushed a darker shade of red.

Mrs. Stewart was surprised by his reaction. "In a printer's file? What kind of confidential material would—"

"It doesn't matter," he snapped. "Just get that file back immediately!"

Mrs. Stewart wasn't used to being spoken to so sharply, and she glared at her boss.

"Never mind. *I'll* do it!" Mr. Laker said as he stormed out to find Karen.

CHAPTER SEVEN

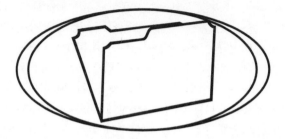

The bell had just rung for the end of the school day. In no time at all, the kids poured out of the classroom, leaving Karen alone with Mrs. Biedermann.

"Is everything all right, Karen?" Mrs. Biedermann asked as she erased the blackboard. "Karen?"

Karen, who was staring at the open file from Mr. Laker's office, jumped. "What?"

"I know my classes are incredibly interesting, but school's out. You can go home now."

Fumbling to close the file and gather her books, Karen mumbled an apology and made her way out of the classroom. Once she was in the hallway, she stopped and opened the file again. *Something is wrong*, she thought.

"Hi, Karen," Lucy said.

Again, Karen jumped. "Don't do that!" she whispered.

"Didn't you see me come up? I was right in front of you."

"No, I didn't," Karen replied, her gaze falling back to the file.

Lucy moved to peer over her shoulder. "Ballistic Printing? What's this?"

"A file from Mr. Laker's office. It's for the printer they use for all the school's forms and stuff," Karen explained. "Mrs. Stewart gave it to me so I could call them about our stationery. I'm supposed to take it back to her."

"Oh. Well, hurry up so we can go home," Lucy said.

Karen didn't move. She continued to flip through the pages in the file. "I nearly forgot I had it," Karen said, as if Lucy had asked her another question. "Then I opened it up to get the phone number, and I saw all these invoices and bids and receipts."

"So?"

Karen looked at Lucy with panic in her eyes. "I wasn't trying to snoop. I just couldn't find the phone number."

"What are you talking about?" Lucy asked. "Who said you were snooping?"

"Nobody—*yet*. But they will if I don't get this file back." Karen started to walk away, but Lucy caught her arm.

"What's wrong, Karen? Why are you acting so weird?" Lucy asked.

"It's probably nothing," Karen said in a tone that meant it was probably something. "It just doesn't make sense, that's all."

Lucy said impatiently, "*What* doesn't make sense?"

Karen looked around to make sure no one was watching, then held up a small stack of forms. "These are bids from last year to print new report-card forms for the school."

"Bids?"

"Yeah, like when you bid at an auction. Except, in this case, printers bid for business."

"I don't get it."

"It's like my stationery. Normally, I would ask two or three companies to give me their best prices on what they'd charge to print everything. When they give me the prices, it's called a *bid*."

Lucy nodded. "Okay, I get it. Then you'd go with whoever cost less, right?"

"Right. But that's what's weird about this file. There are three bids for the report-card forms, but Mr. Laker obviously went with Ballistic Printing, even though they're the most expensive."

"Maybe he has high-class tastes," Lucy suggested.

"But Mr. Felegy made it absolutely clear to me that it was the school board's policy to always go with the lowest price." Again, Karen checked the hallway to make sure they were alone.

Lucy shrugged. "I'm sure Mr. Laker had his reasons."

"I'm sure he did, too," Karen said suspiciously. "Look at this note."

Lucy leaned over and read the typed letter on Ballistic Printing's letterhead. It thanked Mr. Laker for his business, then detailed a lot of form numbers and charges. "What am I supposed to see here?" Lucy asked.

Karen pointed to the PS at the bottom of the letter. "See this?"

Lucy adjusted her glasses and read a handwritten scrawl: "PS—Art, your 'gift' is enclosed as usual for services rendered." The letter was signed "Jim Forrester, President of Ballistic Printing," with a "J. F." scribbled after the PS.

"Gift?"

Karen held up a photocopy of a check for $2,000 payable to Art Laker from Ballistic Printing. Lucy gasped. "Why would Ballistic Printing pay Mr. Laker $2,000?" Karen asked, closing the file.

Lucy's best instincts as a reporter kicked into gear. "Wait a minute," she said. "What we have here is a company that does *all* the school's printing—even though it's *more* expensive—because Mr. Laker is given money by the president." Now it was Lucy's turn to check the hallway. She whispered, "But that's wrong!"

"It sure is," Karen answered.

Now Lucy understood why Karen looked so worried. She had accidentally stumbled onto a small case of corruption in the upper ranks of their school.

"What am I going to do?" Karen asked, then paused thoughtfully. "What would *Jesus* do?"

Lucy put her hand on Karen's shoulder. "I'm not so sure what Jesus would do, but a good reporter would take this file back to the *Owl's* office and make copies of those bids, that letter, and the check!"

****

Lucy and Karen made their way through the *Owl's* office and into the adjoining closet. It was a cramped little room with metal shelving piled high with reams of paper, envelopes, textbooks about journalism, old issues of the *Owl,* and a small photocopier that had been donated to the *Owl* by Mr. Whittaker two years ago. Karen watched nervously while Lucy made copies of the incriminating documents.

"So, what would Jesus do about this?" Lucy asked.

Karen chewed on a fingernail. "I don't know," she said. "Would Jesus have sneaked a peek in the file in the first place?"

"You didn't *sneak* a peek," Lucy rebuked her. "You were looking for a phone number and saw the rest of it by accident. *If* it was an accident."

"What do you mean, *if?* I didn't do this on purpose!"

"I know *you* didn't. But maybe somebody else did."

"Like who?"

"God." Lucy made the last copy and handed the original pages back to Karen. "Mr. Whittaker is always telling us how God answers our prayers in unexpected ways. You said you want to follow in Jesus' steps. Maybe this is His way of testing your pledge."

Karen groaned. "But I thought God was going to show me how to do better on my homework or get along with people I didn't like. I didn't think He'd drop me in the middle of a school scandal!"

"What would Jesus do?" Lucy asked simply.

"I don't know," Karen admitted.

Lucy giggled and said, "Jesus said to go into our closets to pray . . . and this is a closet. So let's pray about it and see what happens."

Karen agreed it was a good idea, and they stood next to the humming copier and prayed for God to help Karen understand what Jesus would do.

"Lucy? Karen? Is anyone in here?" a voice called from the office.

Karen barely stifled a shriek. It was Mr. Laker!

"We're in here," Lucy called back, quickly shoving the copies she'd just made under a package of paper.

"What do I do? What do I say?" Karen asked quickly.

"Just get out of here. We can't let him see us next to the copier!" Lucy whispered and pushed Karen toward the closet door.

Karen stumbled into the *Owl's* office. Mr. Laker was crossing the room and looked at her suspiciously. "Hi," he said. "I've been looking all over for you. Mrs. Biedermann said she saw you with Lucy and had a wild hunch that you'd be here. It looks like her hunch was right."

Lucy came out of the closet and closed the door behind her. "Hi, Mr. Laker," she said pleasantly.

Karen stared at her wordlessly.

"I came to get the Ballistic Printing file," Mr. Laker said. "Do you still have it?"

"Oh, yeah," Karen said and snatched it from her notebook. She handed it over.

"Did you get what you wanted?" asked Mr. Laker.

Karen swallowed hard as her mouth went dry. "Yes, sir. The phone number."

"Good. Y'know, I wasn't very happy with Mrs. Stewart. She shouldn't have let that file out of the office." He patted the file. "Oh, well. No harm done, I guess."

"No, sir," Karen said.

"See you tomorrow then," Mr. Laker said and walked out.

"No harm done," Karen repeated softly.

"*Yet*," Lucy added.

****

Back in his office, Mr. Laker opened the Ballistic Printing file. He hadn't actually looked at its contents for a long time. Invoices, receipts, and letters had been randomly shoved inside without his thinking that anyone else would ever see them. It was one of several files he kept at home. He had a "modified" version of the Ballistic Printing file in the school office—a safer version.

He chastised himself for bringing the file from home. He'd had a meeting with Jim Forrester a few days ago and wanted it on hand. It should have gone back into the filing cabinet at home right away. Obviously, he was getting careless in his old age. Leaving it in his briefcase was stupid. He sighed. He should have cleaned the file out ages ago anyway.

He flipped through the pages, checking each one to see if there was anything unusual—anything that might draw the wrong kind of attention.

The report-card bids caught his eye. What were they doing in there? He thought he'd thrown them away. He swore to himself and laid the bids on the desk. He'd use the office shredder to take care of them.

His gaze drifted back down to the file in his lap. He saw the letter from Jim Forrester, the PS, and the copy of the check—and slammed his fist against the desk.

CHAPTER EIGHT

Whit stood on the long stretch of land behind Whit's End and absentmindedly raked wayward autumn leaves into small piles. His mind was on Raymond Clark. Raking leaves was one of the jobs Whit knew he could have offered the man. He sighed heavily and looked at his watch. It was a little after 3:00 p.m. He knew he needed to hurry, as the after-school rush of kids would keep him busy inside until dinner time. He gazed down at the street in front of his shop just as a young woman—probably in her early twenties—rounded the corner. She stopped when she saw him.

"Hello," she called out.

Whit walked toward her, skirting the shop to lean the rake against the wall. "Hi," he said. "Can I help you?"

As he got closer to the woman, he was struck by her square face and kind eyes—a clear resemblance to Raymond Clark. No doubt it was his daughter.

"Are you John Whittaker?" she asked.

"Yes, I am."

She held out her hand. "I'm Christine Holt—er, *Clark*. You helped my father, I was told. I came to say thank you."

Whit shook her hand. "No thanks are necessary."

"I disagree. You've been extremely kind and generous and—" she stopped as tears came to her abruptly. "I'm sorry," she whispered.

Whit put his arm around her shoulders and led her to the back entrance of the shop. "Come in and sit down," he said. "I'll make us some coffee."

He sat her down at the large, wooden table in the kitchen. Once the coffee had been made and poured, he eased into a chair across from her. She got her tears under control and sat quietly for a moment. Then she explained, "I went to the hospital to identify him and fill out a dozen different forms. When I asked about settling our bill with the doctors, they said you had taken care of everything. So I'm here to settle accounts with you."

Whit sipped his coffee. "There's nothing to settle, Mrs. Holt."

"Christine."

"Christine, then." Whit looked at her earnestly. "I'd be insulted if you insisted on paying me back. I did what I did as a matter of conscience. I only wish I could have done more—and sooner."

"That makes two of us," Christine said, wrapping her fingers around the coffee cup as if to keep them warm. A silent moment passed. "You're wondering how he wound up like he did."

"You don't have to explain anything."

"No, I owe you that much, though I'm not sure about all the details myself." An ironic smile crossed her face. "That must sound terrible coming from his only daughter. But there's so much I didn't know. I'm not even sure where to begin."

"Where are you from?"

"I grew up in Chicago. That's where we lived most of my life. Dad was a press operator for various printers. It was never a great money-making job, but it was all he knew. His father was a printer, too." She lifted the cup to her lips and blew gently across the top to cool the coffee. "All I remember growing up was how little we had. We weren't poverty-stricken, but we were pretty poor. Mom and I did what we could to help out. Dad didn't want us to work, though. He insisted on being the breadwinner of the family. No matter how bad it got, he wouldn't let us find jobs. In fact, he did everything he could to hide how bad things were financially."

"That's how it was with men from the older generation," Whit said.

Christine continued, "I left home to go to college. I worked nights to do it. Dad felt terrible. He kept saying he should pay my tuition. I didn't mind doing it myself. Let's see: That was four years ago. I met Robert on campus—he's my husband—and we moved to Columbus because that's where his work was. He's a legal assistant right now. He's studying to be a lawyer."

"How did your father wind up in Connellsville?" Whit asked.

"The new computer technology kept putting Dad out of work, so he and Mom moved there. Staying in touch got harder and harder from so far away. I wrote and called, but he wouldn't tell me what was happening. He didn't tell me how sick Mom was with cancer. I only found out just before she died. He also didn't mention that he'd lost his job. I kept meaning to come visit him, but we couldn't find the time."

Whit frowned. *Couldn't find the time.* How well he knew that reason. Or was it an excuse? "Why did your father keep so much to himself?"

"He knew I would have insisted that he come live with us in Columbus," Christine said.

"He didn't like Columbus?"

Christine smiled and, for a moment, Whit saw a fresh-faced young girl instead of a grieving daughter. "He didn't want to be a burden to me or Robert."

"If you can't turn to your own family, who can you turn to?" Whit asked softly.

"That's right," Christine said, then lowered her head. "I had no idea he was walking the streets, begging for work. The doctors said he had a very weak heart. If he had only told me—if I'd only known . . ." She clutched a hand to her mouth to stifle a sob.

Whit reached across the table and gently placed his hand over hers.

"I don't know whether I feel sad or extremely angry at

him for hiding so much from me," she said, wiping her nose with a balled-up tissue.

"Tell me about your father's faith. He said a lot of things to us that made me think he was a Christian. Was he?"

Christine nodded. "Oh, yes," she said. "He was an elder in our church for years. That's one thing he didn't hide: his faith. I think he struggled with it sometimes. I know he questioned God when he couldn't keep a job—and when Mom got sick and died. He never said anything outright, just little things that made me believe he was wrestling with what it all meant. The last time I saw him, at Mom's funeral, he asked me if I understood what it really meant to be a Christian. It's as if he was trying to figure out what makes a Christian different from other people. He never said anything judgmental. It was like he was sorting it out for himself."

"He asked us those same questions before he collapsed. It's caused quite a stir. Some of us are doing a lot of soul searching because of him."

"I hope none of you blame yourselves," Christine said. "He was a stranger to you."

Whit looked her directly in the eyes. "He was a stranger, but none of us took him in."

Christine shook her head. "It's not realistic to expect anyone to . . . to . . ."

"Put ourselves on the line like Christians have for the past 2,000 years?"

"You're being too hard on yourself," she replied.

"Not at all. I'm merely asking the same question your

father asked: What does it mean to follow in the footsteps of Jesus? It's an important question to answer."

"*Can* it be answered?" Christine asked.

"Not without great sacrifice, I suspect."

They sat quietly for another moment. The bell above the front door jingled as kids made their way in.

"I think I have some customers," Whit said.

Christine stood up. "My husband is coming tomorrow to help make arrangements for my father. We're going to bury him in Connellsville next to my mother. Will you come to the funeral?"

"Of course," Whit said warmly. "And if you need any help—with *anything*—money or—well, just ask."

Christine took Whit's hand and smiled gratefully. "You've done enough already. Just come to the funeral."

When Tom Riley stopped by to visit later in the evening, Whit told him about his visit with Christine. "She seemed like a very sweet girl," Whit said in conclusion.

"I'm sure she is," Tom said. "I'd like to join you for that funeral, if you don't mind."

"I'd appreciate the company."

Tom climbed onto a stool at the soda counter and eyed his friend. "Well?"

Whit wiped off a table with a damp cloth and picked up someone's sticky, empty ice-cream bowl. "Well what?"

"You've got that pinched look in the corner of your eyes. There's something on your mind," Tom said.

Whit took the dirty dish back to the counter and lingered

there while his mind worked out what he wanted to say. "Tom, this whole thing has done something to me."

"I can see that."

"It's created an ache in my heart that I can't get rid of. And I don't mean feelings of guilt. It's more than that." Whit wiped the counter with the cloth. "Raymond Clark could be any one of us. He was a good man, a *Christian* man, and yet there he was at the end of his life, still wondering what it meant to be a Christian."

"I wonder about it all the time. Don't you?"

Whit shrugged. "I guess I thought I'd have some of it figured out by now. Isn't that one of the benefits of growing old?"

"Says who?" Tom chuckled. "I don't remember anybody giving us guarantees about what we should or shouldn't know. All I remember is that the Bible tells us to be obedient, whether we can figure things out or not."

"I know, I know," Whit said. "But it seems strange to be a Christian as long as I've been and find myself right back at the start. *What would Jesus do?* It's such a basic question, and I've never practiced finding an answer to it."

Tom laughed. "When have you ever had the time, Whit?" he responded. "Look at the hours you put in at this shop—not to mention all the other things you do with the church and various city committees. You're constantly on the run. Not even Jesus tried to do *everything*."

****

The Starduster careened down toward the village of Mythopoeic, its hyper-blast guns trained on the group of unsuspecting citizens going about their business on the main avenue. The Evil Overlord Latas gently squeezed the firing stick. The Starduster jerked as laser balls burst forward. Each one hit the village below, disintegrating the people into clouds of dust and leaving behind craters of black soot. Leisha, daughter of the once-powerful Madrigal, turned and cried for help from the gods of Avaline. Latas trained his sights on her, because she was his only reason for attacking the village in the first place . . .

Matt suddenly paused the video player. "Was that a car door?" he asked. "I thought I heard a car door slam."

"I didn't hear anything. Now turn the tape back on. This is the best part," Jack said, then turned to Oscar, who was hiding his eyes behind a pillow. "You can come out now, Oscar."

Oscar peeked at Jack. "This stuff gives me nightmares. That Overlord Latas and his army remind me of Joe Devlin and his bullies."

Matt listened for a moment to make sure his parents hadn't come home early from their meeting. "I could've sworn I heard them," he said.

"Come on, Matt. This is where Leisha calls down the lightning from Natrom." Jack grabbed for the remote control.

"Wait a minute," Matt said, holding the remote out of Jack's reach.

"What's the matter? Your parents aren't home yet."

"I know, but . . . well, it just suddenly occurred to me that this is wrong."

Jack scrunched his eyebrows down. "*What's* wrong?"

"Watching a movie that I *know* my parents wouldn't want me to watch," answered Matt.

"They didn't say you *couldn't* watch it," Jack reminded him.

"But they didn't say I *could,* either. You brought it over. They don't know anything about it." Matt turned the video off.

Jack groaned. "It's only a movie."

"When Leisha prayed to those gods like she did . . . it seemed wrong. There's only one God," Matt said.

"I was thinking the same thing myself," Oscar chimed in.

Jack folded his arms impatiently. "It's a story that takes place in a different dimension. What's with you guys?"

"We promised that we'd ask what Jesus would do about *everything,*" Matt said. "Would Jesus watch this movie— especially when He didn't have His parents' permission?"

"I don't know," Jack said, shrugging his shoulders. "They didn't have movies when Jesus was a kid."

Matt persisted, "They probably had a lot of things like movies, though. Storytellers or books or whatever. The question is: Would Jesus watch a movie where the bad guys kill everyone and the good guys pray to gods who aren't God?"

"Beats me. How do we find out?"

"Mr. Whittaker said we'd have to study Jesus in the Bible," Oscar offered. "Do you have one around here? I'd like to see what it says about Joe Devlin."

Matt thought about it. "I have a Bible in my room," he said after a moment. "And there's one my dad uses in his den."

They turned off the television, and Jack grabbed the video to put back into his knapsack. He looked at the cover one last time; starships fired at innocent villagers, and a dazzling blonde woman shot lightning from her fingertips at a gruesome monster. For a fleeting second, Jack thought he saw the picture as Jesus would've seen it—and he felt sad. It was only a story, all right, but was it a story Jesus would like? As he slipped the tape into his knapsack, Jack knew he would never watch the film again.

Bibles in hand, the three boys sat down in the living room to see if they could find out what Jesus would do about movies and bullies and anything else they could think of. No one was more surprised by the scene than Matt's parents when they got home.

CHAPTER NINE

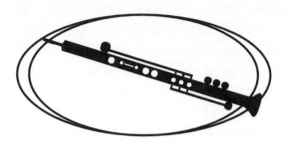

L ucy!" Karen called down the hallway the next morning
at school. "Hi, Karen."
Karen was breathless as she said, "He wants to
see me."

"Who does?" Lucy asked.

"Mr. Laker! He wants to see me in his office," Karen
gasped, looking left and right as if the man himself might be
standing nearby.

Lucy looked at Karen wide-eyed, then fought to keep
control of her own fear. It wouldn't help for both of them to
be panicked. "Really?" she said calmly.

"'Really?' Is that all you can say? What am I going to
do?" Karen asked in a harsh whisper.

"What would Jesus do?"

Karen held her books close to her chest while she rubbed
her eyes wearily with her free hand. "I read my Bible last
night—I prayed—I'm still not sure. Oh, I wish I had never

looked at that stupid file! I didn't get any sleep last night."

"I wonder if Jesus had any sleepless nights from worry?" Lucy asked, more as an accusation than as a question.

Karen frowned at her friend. "Cut it out," she said. "I'm not Jesus. I'm just trying to follow Him. And right now it's scaring me to death."

"Did you tell your parents about the file?"

"No," Karen said quickly. "I'm not ready to do that yet. They'd make me confront Mr. Laker. I don't know if I can do that."

Lucy turned to face Karen. "Jesus exposed the darkness in the world. He got after the religious leaders for leaving God out of all their rules. Isn't it the same here?"

"Maybe it is," Karen said. "But they crucified Jesus in the end, remember?"

"And God raised Him from the dead," Lucy pointed out.

Karen groaned. "But will He raise *me* after Mr. Laker gets done raking me over the coals? I wish I could pretend I didn't see anything. I'm a nervous wreck!"

Lucy ached for her friend but could only say, "I'm sorry, Karen, I want to help you. But I'm not the Holy Spirit. Is there time to go somewhere and pray?"

"No! I have to go meet him *now*."

Lucy scratched her chin thoughtfully. "Maybe Mr. Laker won't even bring it up. You know, he might want to meet you about something else."

Karen looked at her friend hopefully. "Do you really think so?"

"That could be your test. Why don't you wait and see if Mr. Laker brings it up? If he does, you'll probably have to tell him what you know. You can't lie. Jesus wouldn't. But if he *doesn't* mention it, you'll have time to think about what to do. You'll have to tell your parents, you know."

"I know. And I will." Karen backed away from Lucy to go to the office. "Pray for me," she said.

Lucy watched Karen disappear around the corner, then slumped against the wall. She was trying to be strong for her friend. She wanted to encourage her to do the right thing. Yet, in her heart, Lucy was deeply afraid of what Mr. Laker might do to Karen. If he was truly guilty of breaking the school's policy—a policy that was put there for very good reasons—he might try to protect himself. How, though? How far would Mr. Laker go to keep himself out of trouble? The possible answers worried Lucy.

****

Mr. Laker waved to the metal chair just in front of his desk. "Sit down, Karen," he said.

"Yes, sir," Karen said and sat down. She still held her books close, pressing them against her lap.

"I'll come right to the point," he said. "You're an impressive young girl, Karen. Talented, too. You play the oboe, I know."

Karen wasn't sure what to say. Discussing her oboe playing was the last thing she would have expected. "The oboe? Yes, I do," she stammered.

"I heard you at the last school concert. You're quite remarkable."

Karen blushed and said, "Thank you."

"Are you familiar with the Campbell County Youth Orchestra?" he asked, peering at his nails indifferently.

Karen brightened. "Are you kidding? Sure I've heard of it. It's the best there is."

Mr. Laker chuckled and said, "There're probably one or two that are better. But you're right: They're the best in this state for their age group. They take only the brightest students and the most talented players."

"Yes, sir. I hope to play with them one day. Maybe next year."

"How about *this* year?"

Karen tilted her head, unsure of how to take the question. "I beg your pardon?"

Mr. Laker sat forward in his chair again. "Karen, I'm pleased to tell you that you've been selected to play the oboe for the Campbell County Youth Orchestra."

"What?" Karen sat up so quickly that she spilled her books. As she retrieved them from the floor, she asked, "Me? Did you say me? Play for the Campbell County Youth Orchestra?"

Mr. Laker nodded his head happily. "It's a paid position, with money going to your future education. You know the orchestra's sterling reputation, of course—not to mention the many opportunities it presents."

Karen was genuinely stunned. "I don't know what to say, Mr. Laker!" she managed to utter. "How did it happen? I mean, why did they suddenly choose me?"

"They had an unexpected opening, and . . ." He paused and looked away as if he were suddenly embarrassed. "I shouldn't say."

"Shouldn't say what?"

"Well, I'm a member of the orchestra's selection committee. I put your name forward as a candidate. Just last night, as a matter of fact. The rest of the committee agreed unanimously."

"I can't believe this!" Karen squealed and nearly dropped her books again.

He raised a finger. "Oh—there's only one tiny drawback."

"Drawback?" she asked anxiously.

"Yes," he said. "You'll have to resign as president of the student council. The orchestra puts in an awful lot of practice hours, you know. That's why they're so good. You wouldn't have time for both."

Karen was instantly awash with relief. "Is that all?" she said. "Who cares about being on the student council when I can perform with the orchestra?"

"I thought as much," Mr. Laker said with a smile.

In her excitement, Karen suddenly wondered why she had always been so afraid of Mr. Laker. *He's a* nice *man*, she thought. She'd misjudged him. Maybe even the file had an easy explanation; it was a mistake; she had misunderstood what she saw. Who cared about it now anyway? *She was going to play for the Campbell County Youth Orchestra!*

Unexpectedly, a small voice whispered in the back of her mind: *What would Jesus do?*

The answer this time seemed obvious to her. Jesus would use His God-given talents to play for the orchestra. It wasn't as if being president of the student council had anything to do with her future anyway. Jesus would say yes.

Would He? The question made her terribly uncomfortable.

Mr. Laker's smile faded. "Karen?"

"I need to talk to my parents," she suddenly heard herself saying. Even as the words came out, she wanted to stop them. She was afraid he'd take the offer back just because she didn't say yes right away.

"I'd never let you do it without talking to your parents first."

"Thank you, Mr. Laker." She stood up to leave and said again awkwardly, "Thank you."

"You're welcome." He thrust his hand out to her, and she shook it.

It was cold and clammy. A chill went up and down her spine.

CHAPTER TEN

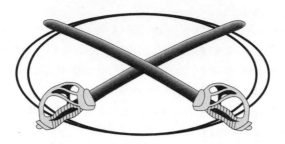

Jack finished the last of his french fries and pushed the plate and cafeteria tray aside. Matt was still eating his hamburger.

"Where's Oscar?" asked Jack, scanning the large room and all the students who were eating their lunches.

Matt glanced around. "Is today when he meets Mrs. McKenzie in the library?" he asked. "She's been helping him with his reading lately."

"Nope."

Joe Devlin, a large kid with greasy, dark hair, walked up to the table with a lunch tray. He was followed by a couple of the members of his gang whose sole purpose in life was to laugh at his jokes and win his fights. "It's the Bobbsey Twins," Joe said to Jack and Matt.

Joe's pals snickered obediently.

"And you must be the Three Stooges," Matt said.

"Do we want to make these two clowns move so we can

sit here, boys?" Joc asked his cohorts.

"You'll have to wait until I'm finished eating," Matt said.

Joe reached over and shoved his forefinger through the top of Matt's hamburger. "Feels cold," he said with a smirk. "You don't want to eat the rest of that anyway. Get lost."

Matt leaped to his feet. "That's not funny, Joe!" he said.

"You gonna do something about it?" Joe challenged him.

"Yeah," Matt sneered, then grabbed the hamburger off Joe's tray and took a bite out of it.

"Hey!" Joe shouted and slammed his tray down on the table.

Matt laughed at him until Jack suddenly said, "What would Jesus do, Matt?"

That was enough to stop Matt—and Joe, who turned to Jack and asked, "What did you say?"

"Is everything all right here?" a deep baritone voice asked. It was their principal, Mr. Felegy. He stood well over six feet tall, with a barrel chest, thin, sandy-brown hair, and piercing eyes that defied anyone to rebel against his authority.

"Yes, sir," each of them mumbled.

"Then I suggest you find a table and eat your lunch before the bell rings," he said, and he was gone as quickly as he'd arrived.

Joe forced a chuckle. "It's okay," he said. "Keep the hamburger. I have plenty of money for another lunch today, compliments of the First Bank of Oscar." He laughed viciously, and his two friends cackled with him as they walked off.

Jack and Matt exchanged looks as the meaning of Joe's words sank in. They raced out of the cafeteria.

****

Jack and Matt found Oscar at the end of the hallway behind the gym. He sat with his arms wrapped around his bent knees and rocked slightly.

"Oscar!" Matt called out as they got closer.

"Are you all right?" asked Jack.

He looked up at them with pain in his eyes.

Matt knelt next to him. "Did they hurt you?"

He shook his head no.

"Then what happened? They got your lunch money, right?" Jack asked.

He nodded.

Matt looked him over. "But they didn't beat you up. You just *gave* it to them?"

He nodded again, then buried his face in his arms and cried softly.

"Aw, don't do that," Jack said as he sat down next to him.

Oscar sniffled, "You don't know what it's like. They pick on me all the time, no matter where I am. They don't even have to beat me up anymore. I just give them what they want so they'll go away."

Matt clenched and unclenched his fists. "I'm getting pretty tired of Joe," he said. "I think it's time he got taught a lesson."

"No," Oscar said, then lifted his head and spoke louder. "No. You can't do anything."

"Who says we can't?" Jack growled.

Oscar looked at Matt, then Jack, and said, "Would Jesus get revenge?"

Jack groaned. Matt hit his fist against the floor and complained, "I *knew* you were going to say that!"

"We made a promise," Oscar reminded them. "What would Jesus do about this?"

"I wish we never went to that meeting," Jack said under his breath.

Matt stood up and paced angrily. "I won't ever make a promise—ever again."

"I thought you guys were Christians," Oscar said.

"Don't start preaching to us, Oscar," Jack said. "It's bad enough that I didn't see the rest of my movie last night."

Oscar shook his head. "I'm not preaching. I'm just saying that we promised to try to follow Jesus. Why did we spend two hours reading through the Bible last night? What did we say? We said that Jesus knew what He was talking about and we should listen to Him."

Matt looked at Jack and spread his hands. "He's preaching to us anyway."

Oscar slowly got to his feet. "Getting revenge isn't what Jesus would do. He said to turn the other cheek. He said to pray for guys who persecute us. He said that people who live by the sword die by the sword."

"My dad has a Civil War sword in his den," Matt said

thoughtfully, as if he meant to use it on Joe.

"So what do you suggest, Reverend Oscar?" Jack asked irritably. "How are we going to stop Joe Devlin? You'll never eat another lunch as long as he's around. Unless you want to tell on him."

"No!" Oscar said. "I don't want to be teased for being a tattletale. Besides, he'll just pick on me when the teachers aren't around."

"So what should we do?" Matt asked. "This isn't right!"

Oscar looked at Matt and Jack and said sincerely, "Don't do anything. Don't even say anything."

"I don't get it," Jack said.

Oscar picked up his school books. "Remember? Jesus didn't say anything to those guys who crucified Him. He didn't fight back. He didn't argue. That's what I'm going to try with Joe and his gang. I won't fight back, and I won't fuss. He may get what he wants from me, but it won't be any fun for him."

****

Though it was a cool autumn day, Lucy and Karen ate their lunches on the patio behind the cafeteria. The air had a hint of winter around its edges, as if it were snowing somewhere far away. Lucy pulled her jacket around her.

"So, they don't like any of your ideas?" Karen asked Lucy. They had been talking about Lucy's meeting that morning with the staff of the *Owl*.

"They think I'm crazy."

Karen shook her head. "You want to do positive articles. You want to have a more healthy attitude about the news. Why is it crazy to want to do *good* things?"

"Because they don't understand," Lucy said. She put her sandwich down on the plastic wrap that served as a plate. "I've been thinking about it a lot this morning. Y'know, I don't *really* know any of the kids I work with. I don't know if any of them are Christians."

"Mike is, isn't he?"

Lucy shrugged. "I don't know for sure. Funny, he's probably the loudest about me being out of my mind. He said I should resign before I ruin everything and lose all our readers."

"Don't listen to him."

"But I know why he's so mad," Lucy said. "I understand how they feel. I'd feel the same way if Mrs. Stegner suddenly walked in and said, 'I'm a Buddhist, and I want the *Owl* to write about Buddhist ideas.'"

"That's not what you're doing," said Karen.

"I'm sure it seems like it to them. Out of the blue, I come marching in with a whole different way of doing things, and it's like I'm forcing everyone to follow what I believe." Lucy nibbled at her sandwich, lost in her thoughts, then said, "You see, when Jesus went into various towns and villages, they didn't know who He was. But when they heard the kinds of things He said, and saw the love He had and the way He healed people, they figured He was someone to listen to.

What am I showing the staff of the *Owl?* It's not like I took time to get to know them or do anything except throw my beliefs at them."

"What were you supposed to do, walk on water? Heal their acne?"

"Somehow I should've shown that I *care* about them—the way Jesus cared. Then maybe they'd be more open to my ideas."

A somber silence followed for a minute. Both girls seemed to realize the significance of what Lucy was trying to do. The stakes were high. It was entirely possible that it would end with Lucy having to resign.

"Forget about the *Owl,*" Lucy abruptly said. "I want to hear *your* news. You've been busting to tell me ever since we sat down, and I haven't given you the chance."

Karen looked at her coolly. "Oh, it's nothing special," she said.

Lucy raised her eyebrow like a question mark.

With growing excitement, Karen said, "It's only that Mr. Laker has asked me to play oboe with the Campbell County Youth Orchestra!"

Lucy dropped her sandwich. "What?" she squeaked. "Is that why he wanted to see you?"

Karen nodded quickly. "Yeah! Isn't that great?"

"Congratulations!" Lucy said as she half-hugged Karen across the table.

"The only problem is that I'd have to resign as president of the student council. But I don't care. Though . . ."

"Though what?"

"I remembered to stop and ask myself what Jesus would do," Karen said proudly. "So I didn't tell Mr. Laker yes or no."

"Good for you. What do you think Jesus would do?"

As with so many situations they'd already encountered, Karen gave the standard answer: "I don't know. Would Jesus play for an orchestra? Would He use His talents like that? We keep running into this same brick wall. 'What would Jesus do?' 'I don't know.' It's enough to drive me crazy. I didn't realize how ignorant I was about Jesus until now."

Lucy took her glasses off and cleaned them with a napkin. "There's something else to consider," she said. "What if Mr. Laker is doing this to cover himself?"

Karen said she didn't understand.

"What if he's afraid you looked through the file?" Lucy asked. "What if he's doing this to sort of bribe you to keep your mouth shut?"

Karen's face fell. "I hadn't thought of that," she admitted.

Lucy said, "Just because he got you a place on the orchestra doesn't mean you should forget what you saw."

Karen blushed. Whether she meant to or not, she *had* put the file out of her mind. She was ready to drop it. "Oh, Lucy," she said in despair, "what *are* we going to do? If I blow the whistle now, I'll never get to play with the orchestra."

"If you blow the whistle, some people will call you a tattletale," Lucy added. "You could lose your position as president of the student council, too."

Karen put her face in her hands. "What am I going to do?"

Lucy gently touched her arm. "Maybe it's time we went back to Mr. Whittaker and asked him about some of this stuff. He's the one who started this situation in the first place. He might have some answers."

Karen agreed. "Let's go after school."

****

Heather Carr caught Karen just as she was headed out the door after school. "I've been looking for you," Heather said. They were best friends, though Karen hadn't seen her since the "pledge."

"Hi, Heather," Karen said. "Sorry, but I have to go. I'm late." She was in a rush to get to Whit's End, where she was meeting Lucy. She had also bumped into Jack, Oscar, and Matt earlier in the hall, and they had agreed to go to Whit's End for a few answers of their own.

"A bunch of us are going to the mall," Heather said. She sounded annoyed. "Do you want to come with us?"

Karen replied, "I can't. I have a meeting."

"With who? *Lucy?*" The accusation was unmistakable.

"Yeah, with Lucy. Why?"

"It just seems like you've been hanging out with her a lot. You don't have time left for your *old* friends—like me."

"Cut it out, Heather." Karen didn't have the patience for this encounter, but she wanted to explain anyway. "Weren't you in church last Sunday?"

"No. I was out of town, remember? I told you we were going to my grandmother's."

"I forgot. Sorry. Anyway, some of us made a commitment to do everything the way Jesus would do it, and it has . . . complicated things."

"I've heard all about the complications some of you guys are having," Heather countered. "And I heard that you were offered the chance to play oboe for the orchestra. Thanks for telling me yourself. Do you know how embarrassing it is to learn that your *best friend* had something exciting happen and didn't tell you? But now that you're part of this holier-than-thou club, I guess it's too much to expect."

Karen grimaced. "I'm sorry, Heather. I was going to tell you myself, but I haven't seen you. Besides, I don't know that I'm going to do it."

"Too good for the orchestra now?" Heather asked snippily.

"Give me a break. That's not it. Look, why don't you come with me to Whit's End? Then you can see what we're talking about."

"No, thanks. I already told the rest of the girls I'd meet them at the mall. Jesus would want me to keep my commitments, wouldn't He?" She grinned sarcastically, turned on her heel, and walked off.

"Heather, wait!" Karen called out. "You don't understand."

Heather didn't look back or respond.

Karen grumbled under her breath, then remembered the many friends and family members whom Jesus had lost due to misunderstanding. She made her way toward Whit's End.

CHAPTER ELEVEN

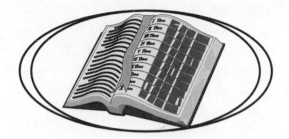

So, what would you like to talk about?" Whit asked as he turned the sign on the front door of Whit's End so the "Closed—Be Back in 30 Minutes" faced outside. He didn't want this meeting to be disturbed. "Well? Things aren't going the way you thought?"

The five of them—Lucy, Karen, Jack, Matt, and Oscar— looked at each other across the table where they had gathered. No one knew who should speak first.

Lucy cleared her throat, then said, "One of the biggest problems is that we don't know Jesus well enough to figure out what He'd do."

Whit sat down at the table with them. "We said from the start that that might be a problem. We have to know Him to follow Him. But He didn't leave us high and dry. We have the Bible and the Holy Spirit."

"It's not helping," Matt complained. "We spent hours looking through the Bible last night, and Oscar still got robbed by Joe Devlin."

Whit turned to Oscar. "Do you want me to talk to Joe's parents?" he asked.

"No," Oscar said. "It won't help. Unless you give me police protection 24 hours a day, Joe will get to me somehow."

"Mr. Whittaker," Karen said, "it might sound a little weird, but we don't want you to do *anything* about what we have to say. We just need you to listen and . . . give us some advice."

He looked into the faces of the five kids, then nodded. "Okay. But I reserve the right to *advise* you to talk to your parents. Now, let's take this one at a time. Joe Devlin keeps picking on Oscar. What would Jesus do about that?"

"Hit Joe with lightning bolts from heaven," Matt suggested.

"Hardly."

Jack chimed in: "Jesus said to turn the other cheek, and now Oscar's got some wacko idea to . . ." He hooked his thumb at Oscar. "You tell him, Oscar, and see what he thinks."

Oscar explained to Whit that he thought he should act as Jesus did before they crucified Him. "He didn't argue, He didn't fight back, so that's what I'm going to do with Joe. I'll keep my mouth shut and won't do anything."

Whit stroked his mustache as he considered the idea. Finally he said, "For 2,000 years, people have tried to decide what Jesus meant by 'Turn the other cheek.' And for that same amount of time, kids have been dealing with bullies and wondering if what Jesus said applied to their situation. I've talked to some parents who say that the only way to lick a bully is to knock him flat."

"Yeah!" Matt said.

"Other people think that fighting only begets more fighting until someone gets *really* hurt." Whit gazed at Oscar. "Chances are, you couldn't knock Joe flat, right?"

"Nope," Oscar replied.

"Then you should try your plan to see if it works. What have you got to lose?" Whit concluded.

"Is that it?" Jack asked. *"That's* how you figure out what Jesus would do?"

"Following Jesus doesn't mean you throw away your good sense, Jack," said Whit. "You've studied your Bibles, you've explored what Jesus said, and now you're putting it into action. This is what Oscar believes he should do. It's *his* decision—not yours or Matt's. God will honor what's in his heart."

Both Jack and Matt slid down in their chairs and folded their arms. They didn't agree but kept their mouths shut.

Whit looked at Lucy. "How are you doing, Lucy?" he asked.

Lucy shrugged. "Okay, I guess," she answered. "I didn't realize this little experiment would make me feel so . . . so *alone.* I've got everybody on the *Owl's* staff against me."

"But you've got *God* for you," Whit said with a smile. "And we're with you in this, too. To listen, to pray . . ."

"Yeah, I know. And I appreciate it." Lucy hesitated, then

asked, "Do you think Jesus ever felt alone?"

The kindness in Whit's eyes seemed to sparkle as he looked at Lucy and said, "I'm sure He did sometimes. In the Garden of Gethsemane, Jesus was probably the loneliest person in all of history. But He still said, 'Thy will be done.'"

Somewhere a clock ticked, and one of the ice cream freezers rattled and hummed.

"Karen?" Whit asked.

"It's lonely," she said. "And people don't understand why we're doing this. They think we're trying to be better than everyone else."

"Misunderstanding is part of it," Whit said. "They misunderstood Jesus, and they've misunderstood His followers for 2,000 years. More often than not, we're perfectly understood and they *still* don't like what we stand for."

"Isn't there something else you want to say, Karen?" asked Lucy.

"No. I don't have anything else right now," she said.

Lucy looked surprised. "You don't?"

"No," Karen said simply, then glanced away.

Whit observed the unspoken argument going on between the girls, then said as if to change the subject, "Would it help if we met like this more often? I get together with some of the adults who made the pledge every couple of days. Mostly we pray. Would you like to do that?"

Each of them mumbled their assent.

Whit chuckled to himself. *Their enthusiasm is breathtaking*, he thought. "Let's spend a little time in prayer, and then I need to open the shop again," he said.

They bowed their heads.

****

"What happened?" Lucy asked Karen as they walked down the sidewalk away from Whit's End. "Why didn't you tell Mr. Whittaker about Mr. Laker?"

"I didn't need to. I know what I have to do," Karen said.

"What?"

"The thing I was supposed to do all along."

Lucy navigated a step in front of Karen and stood directly in her way. "*What* are you going to do?"

Karen answered on the verge of tears, "Did you hear what he said about Jesus? He was all alone in the Garden of Gethsemane. He gave up everything He had—even His life— to do God's will. Why am I worried about playing for an orchestra? Why should I care if I'm president of the student council? 'Thy will be done,' He said. Those words burned inside me." Karen fought to hold back a sob. "I've known all along what I was supposed to do, but I was being a coward. I won't be one anymore."

The dam of tears broke. Karen pushed past Lucy and ran down the sidewalk.

CHAPTER TWELVE

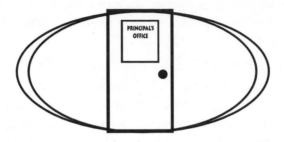

First thing the next morning, Karen found herself pacing back and forth in front of Mr. Laker's office door. He walked in through the main door, dressed in a heavy coat and furry hat. He stopped suddenly when he saw her. "Hi, Karen," he said. "What are you doing here?"

"I need to talk to you, Mr. Laker."

"About the orchestra," he said as he shoved his key into the door lock. He pushed the door open. "Come in."

She followed him in, her stomach churning nervously. Did Jesus feel this way when He confronted the Pharisees? Did He want to throw up when He stood before Pilate?

Mr. Laker hung his coat and hat on the coat rack. "Did you talk to your parents?" he asked.

"No, sir. Not yet," she said, then swallowed hard. Oh *why* hadn't she talked to her parents first? She was afraid to, that's why. She thought her dad would make a federal case out of it. She imagined him calling the police and making her go to court and sit on the witness stand. This way, she could talk to Mr. Laker alone, and maybe he'd confess and promise to make amends, and then she could forget about the whole thing.

Mr. Laker watched Karen for a moment. "Why not?" he asked.

"Because I wanted to talk to you again first."

"Oh?"

"Yes, sir." She paused, wishing she had a glass of water. "I'm sorry, but I have to say no about the orchestra."

Mr. Laker looked genuinely disappointed. "That's too bad," he said. "You'd be a wonderful asset to them, I'm sure. Why won't you do it?"

"Because . . . I'm afraid there's a price tag attached to it that I can't afford."

"A price tag? What kind of price tag?"

She'd practiced the speech a hundred times that morning. None of the words came to mind. "Let's see . . . does the word *bribery* mean anything to you?"

He blinked a couple of times but kept his face solidly straight. "You think I bribed someone to get you on the orchestra?"

Karen tugged at her collar. It seemed awfully hot all of a sudden. "Mr. Laker, I don't know how to start. I saw some things in the Ballistic Printing file that you probably didn't want me to see."

"Like what?"

"Well . . ."

"Shall I get the file for you? Maybe that'll help." He

opened the large filing cabinet drawer and pulled out a manila folder. "You have me worried, Karen. You're acting like something is seriously wrong."

He handed the file to her. She was stunned by his behavior and didn't know what to make of it. Was it some kind of trick? Did he *want* to get in trouble? She opened the file and worked through the various documents. The papers looked similar but not identical to the ones she'd seen before. In less than a minute, she'd reached the bottom. The bids, the letter, and the copy of the check were gone.

"You took them out," she said.

"Took what out?"

"Those bids—and the letter—and the check."

"Bids? Letter? Check?"

Karen turned red. "There were bids in here to print our report cards. Two printers were cheaper than Ballistic Printing, but you went with Ballistic anyway. It's against school board policy to go with a more expensive printer when you have *two* who are less expensive."

Mr. Laker chuckled and said, "I think you must be feverish, Karen. Do you want me to call the school nurse?"

"No, sir." She took a deep breath to control her quivering voice. "You took a bribe, Mr. Laker. I saw the PS on the letter about your so-called gift. And I saw the check. Why would they pay you $2,000 unless it was to keep your business?"

Mr. Laker's cheeks pinkened; then he forced a smile. "You don't know what you're getting into, Karen."

"I . . . I want you to admit to what you did and talk to Mr.

Felegy. Maybe they won't fire you," she said, trying to stick to her plan.

"Maybe they'll send me to bed without my supper," Mr. Laker said, laughing. "I don't know what you're talking about. And you can see for yourself that there's no letter or check in the file."

"They were there, and you know it!" she shouted.

"Don't get hysterical," he urged.

"You got rid of the evidence! I saw them with my own two eyes!"

"Then you'd better get your eyes checked."

Karen's mouth moved, but nothing came out. She could insist over and over, but it wouldn't make any difference without proof.

"Now, can we stop this nonsense, please?" he said.

In the main office area, a door slammed. Someone had arrived. "Good morning!" Mrs. Stewart called from the other room. Karen could hear her drop her purse on the desk.

Mr. Laker spoke louder, as if having a new witness were important. "I don't know what your problem is, Karen," he said. "I tried to do something nice for you by getting you on the orchestra, and this is how you say thanks. I feel sorry for you. You need to see a counselor, get some help."

"But . . . but . . ."

"There's nothing left to say. You're going to be late for class."

Karen turned to leave. All the feeling in her mind and body seemed to disappear.

"Karen," Mr. Laker added in a low voice, "you're in over your head with things you know very little about. I'd keep my lips sealed if I were you. Wild accusations will only come back to hurt *you*. Do you understand?"

****

Lucy discovered Karen crying in a restroom stall. Recognizing her shoes under the short, gray door, Lucy knocked softly. "Karen," she whispered.

The sniffling from the other side of the door suddenly stopped. "Lucy?"

"Yeah, it's me."

The door jerked open, and Karen threw herself into Lucy's arms. "It was awful!" she said. "Awful!"

"What was?" Lucy held her tight for a moment, then gently pushed her back to arm's length. "You have to hurry and tell me. The bell's about to ring."

Karen dabbed at her eyes with some toilet tissue. "I talked to Mr. Laker."

"This *morning?* Why didn't you tell me?"

"I wanted to handle it myself—like Jesus did." Karen walked over to the sink and despaired of her looks. Her eyes were puffy, and her nose was rubbed raw from the cheap toilet tissue.

"What happened?" Lucy asked as she watched Karen get herself straightened up.

"He had cleaned the file out," Karen said. "In fact, I'm

not even sure it was the *same* file we saw. I looked like an idiot."

Lucy leaned against the sink and folded her arms. "What did you think he'd do, break under the truth and confess everything?"

"Yeah, I guess maybe I did," Karen said, half-smiling. "But he denied everything and said I was an ingrate and needed to see a counselor and . . . and it's all true! I must've been crazy. What could I do without any proof?"

"Did you tell him about the copies?"

"Copies?"

"The copies we made," Lucy said. "Remember?"

Karen pressed her hand to her mouth from shock and embarrassment. "My brains have been so tied up that I forgot all about them! I kept thinking about what Jesus would do. And I didn't think Jesus would ever need *proof*."

"Oh, Karen . . ." Lucy put her head in her hands and shook her head.

"Where are they?" Karen asked, grabbing for this shred of hope.

"I gave them to you," Lucy said.

"You did?" She thought about it a moment. "No, you didn't. You kept them."

"Honest, Karen, I don't have them. Check your desk, your notebooks, *everywhere.* You must have hidden them."

Karen looked panicked again. "But I didn't. You made the copies and kept them with you! I'd remember!"

Lucy eyed her skeptically. "How could you remember

that when you didn't even remember there were copies at all?"

"Don't yell at me," Karen said. "I'm feeling fragile right now."

Lucy groaned. "Okay. Maybe I'm wrong. Let's *both* check. One of us hid them somewhere!"

****

"Hey, look! It's our old buddy Oscar!"

Oscar stopped on the playground and turned to face Joe Devlin and his gang. Out of the corner of his eye, Oscar saw Jack and Matt step through the door into the school building with the rest of the class. Joe and his pals surrounded Oscar as they always did.

"How's it going, Osc?" Joe asked as he poked a finger into Oscar's shoulder. "Did you have fun playing soccer in P. E.?"

Oscar took a deep breath, then merely gazed at him.

"What's the matter, cat got your tongue?" Joe laughed. The gang chortled with him.

Oscar didn't reply. He simply looked at Joe and waited.

Joe eyed him carefully. "What's the matter with you? You got laryngitis? Say something."

Oscar didn't move, didn't twitch a face muscle, didn't react at all.

Joe pushed him. "I said *say something*."

Oscar stared at Joe like a little lamb.

"You heard him," one of the other gang members suddenly

said from the side, and he shoved Oscar in another direction. "Speak!"

Still no sound from Oscar.

The gang began to taunt him, pushing and jabbing from all sides until he bounced between them like a pinball in a machine. Still, he didn't say a word. When they tired of that little game, Joe grabbed Oscar by the front of his shirt and pulled him close.

"Say something," he hissed.

Oscar looked into his eyes but wouldn't obey.

Joe thrust him away. "This is getting on my nerves. I'm tempted to give you a good pounding for being so rude."

Oscar reached into his pocket and silently held out his lunch money.

Joe slapped the money away. "I don't want your stupid money," he growled. "I want you to *talk to me!*"

Oscar continued to look at him without a sound.

Clenching his fists, Joe stepped forward as if he might slug Oscar. "That's it!"

Oscar closed his eyes and waited for the blow.

It never came. Joe snarled, then spun on his heel and marched away. With a few extra shoves for good measure, Joe's pals brushed past Oscar and followed their leader across the playground toward the school.

Oscar slowly slumped to the ground, tense from fear but happy at the same time. He slowly picked up his money.

At lunch, Jack and Matt weren't as pleased as Oscar about the encounter with Joe.

"He still pushed you around," Jack complained.

Matt agreed. "The point is, his bullying has got to *stop!*"

Oscar swallowed a bite of bologna sandwich. "But I think it *will* stop," he said. "Even if it doesn't, I'm still doing what I think Jesus would do, and that makes me feel *great.* I got to keep my lunch money, too!"

"I don't care," Jack said. He and Matt looked at one another.

Matt nodded with understanding. "Okay, this afternoon."

Oscar peered at Jack, then Matt, then asked, "This afternoon? What about this afternoon?"

"None of your business," Matt said.

"What are you guys up to?" Oscar asked, instantly worried. "Remember: What would Jesus do?"

Jack leaned toward Oscar and told him, "You just leave it to us."

Matt also leaned forward and added with a smile, "Don't forget that Jesus made whips and drove the money changers out of the temple."

****

"Did you find the copies?" Karen asked Lucy anxiously when they sat down at lunch.

"No. I guess you didn't either, huh?"

Karen shook her head. "No sign of them. What did we do with them, Lucy?"

"You didn't take them home, did you?"

"I don't remember ever having them! How could I know if I took them home?" Karen asked.

"Well, I know *I* didn't," Lucy said.

"Maybe Mr. Laker will forget I ever brought it up," Karen wished. "Without those copies, I'm just an insane kid who makes stupid accusations."

"Uh oh," Lucy said, looking over Karen's shoulder.

Karen turned and saw Mrs. Stewart crossing the cafeteria toward her. A sinking feeling worked through her stomach.

Mrs. Stewart arrived. Her face looked pinched and worried. "Mr. Felegy wants to see you right away," she said.

Karen shot a parting glance at Lucy and followed Mrs. Stewart out of the cafeteria.

"Thank you for coming so fast," Mr. Felegy said when Karen got to his office and had taken a seat.

Karen nodded and said, "You're welcome." She wondered if Mr. Laker had said something to Mr. Felegy about their conversation that morning and clung tightly to the arms of the chair.

"This is a little awkward, Karen," Mr. Felegy continued. "You're a student that I trust and hold in great respect. For those reasons, I thought I'd talk to you before I called your parents."

"Call my parents? But—why?"

Mr. Felegy handed her a computer print-out. At the top, it said, "Student Council Finance Statement." Underneath were columns of figures related to how the student council had been spending its small budget. Karen recognized the form.

As president, she had to be familiar with it, but she couldn't imagine why Mr. Felegy was showing it to her. "You know this?" he asked.

"Yes, sir."

"Then perhaps you can explain that bottom line. The one that says, 'Miscellaneous Expenses.'"

She looked down the page until she came to the phrase. Next to it was the figure "$347.00," and in parentheses it said, "(Karen Crosby)."

"I don't know what that means," Karen said.

"Don't you?" Mr. Felegy asked. "It means that you personally spent $347 on something, but we can't find out what it was. There are no records in the student council files except for a receipt showing you'd taken the money out of the account. Think, Karen. Why did you need the money?"

Karen worked through her memory for any time or reason she may have used money from the student council funds. "I had posters made for the charity car wash . . . the walk-a-thon . . . the fundraiser for the trip to Chicago . . ."

"All those expenses are accounted for elsewhere," Mr. Felegy said.

Karen was at a loss. She couldn't remember spending as much as $347 on anything. Even if she had, she would have filed the receipts so that a strict accounting could be made. "I don't know, Mr. Felegy," she said. "Why did this come up?"

"The school is being audited by the district office, and Mr. Laker pointed out that—"

"Mr. Laker?"

Mr. Felegy explained, "As school administrator, he's in charge of all the finances. You know that."

"I know, but . . . did *he* bring this to you?"

"Yes. He said he didn't consider it a major problem, except that it seemed irregular. But *I* consider it a problem when $347 disappears from the student council funds and we don't know where it went." He kept his gaze fixed on her.

"Mr. Laker keeps all this stuff on his computer?" she asked.

"Yes."

Suddenly it clicked into place. Karen bit her nail and thought it through: Mr. Laker must have somehow juggled the figures on his computer. But did she dare say so to Mr. Felegy? Perhaps this was the moment of truth. What choice did she have?

"Karen, it's an awful lot of money, and I certainly don't consider you irresponsible. But I need you to think very hard and tell me where you spent it."

"I didn't," Karen said, working up to her confession.

"Then who did?"

"I don't know, but it wasn't me," she said. "Maybe nobody spent it. Maybe it was never there."

Mr. Felegy looked at her quizzically. "Explain, please," he ordered.

"Well," Karen began slowly, "I work on our computer at home with my dad. I've seen him do our finances. Last April, he pulled a joke on my mom by putting in the computer that she had spent $1,000 on groceries in one day."

Mr. Felegy frowned and said, "Why are you telling me this story?"

"Because I think Mr. Laker put in a bogus figure to get me in trouble." There. It was out in the open.

Mr. Felegy pushed back from his desk and looked at her with a strained calmness. "Why would Mr. Laker want to get you in trouble?" he asked.

"Because I was going to get *him* in trouble."

"Oh boy," Mr. Felegy groaned. "I don't like the sound of *that*. You'd better tell me everything."

So Karen did: from when Mrs. Stewart gave her the file until her conversation with Mr. Laker that morning. It sounded almost ridiculous even to Karen's ears, but it was the truth, and it had to be said.

"These are serious accusations, Karen," Mr. Felegy said after a long pause.

"I know."

"Do you have any proof?" he asked.

Karen cringed. "I knew you were going to ask me that."

"Well?"

"I *do* have proof," Karen said. "Somewhere. I just can't find it."

Mr. Felegy sighed. "Karen, you're putting me in a very difficult position. I've got a computer print-out that shows you spent $347 that wasn't yours to spend, and you're telling me Mr. Laker is on the 'take' with our best printing company, but you don't have proof. Do you realize how this looks?"

"Yes, sir."

"How do you suggest I proceed?" he asked.

Karen closed her eyes and prayed for a miracle. "Let's get Lucy. Maybe she found the copies we made of the documents in his file."

CHAPTER THIRTEEN

Lucy was having problems of her own. After lunch, she went to the *Odyssey Owl* office to make sure their next issue was coming together the way she'd hoped. Three of the *Owl's* reporters—Mike, Sean Campbell, and Debbie Calhoun—were gathered around the table, talking in low, conspiratorial voices with Mrs. Stegner.

"What's going on?" Lucy asked.

Startled, they spun around.

Lucy approached them. "Come on, guys. What're you talking about?"

"A friend of yours," Mrs. Stegner said.

"*Which* friend?" Lucy asked.

"Karen," Mike replied, and he handed her two sheets of notepaper.

Lucy looked down at the pages. The first was an accounting of the student council's funds. Highlighted in yellow was an entry that read, "Miscellaneous Expenses:

$347.00 (Karen Crosby)." She didn't know what to make of it. "So?" she asked.

"Keep reading," Mike said. He had a smile on his face, but it wasn't friendly. He seemed to be taking pleasure from Lucy's ignorance.

Lucy held up the other page. It was a plain sheet of paper with a note typed to Mike:

> Mike,
> You're the "hot" investigative reporter for the *Owl,* so this information will be interesting to you. There's a deficit in the student council funds. (See highlight on the next page.) It's obvious who took the money. Maybe your editor knows her, too. Worth a story?
> — An Anonymous Friend

That's why Karen got called to the office, Lucy thought. She was dumbfounded. This was the kind of thing that happened to big-city newspapers, not little school papers. "A news leak?" she said. "A news leak in our school?"

"Interesting, isn't it?" Mrs. Stegner said.

"Well, Miss Crusading, Truth-Finding Editor, can I do an article about it?" Mike asked.

"No!" Lucy snapped.

Mike gestured to Mrs. Stegner, Sean, and Debbie. "What did I say?" he said. "She's going to cover for her friend."

Lucy turned on Mike. "I'm not covering for anybody!" she

insisted. "For one thing, Karen wouldn't steal the council's money. For another thing, we don't have any evidence besides this anonymous note and the treasury report!"

"Those are two pretty good pieces of evidence," Debbie said. "What more do we need?"

"These aren't *facts,* they're circumstantial evidence." Lucy appealed to Mrs. Stegner. "I'm right, aren't I? We can't write an article *speculating* about missing money and then suggest that Karen took it. Since when do we write about *any* of our fellow students like that? We're a school newspaper, not muckrakers!"

"What do we do then?" Mrs. Stegner asked.

"Nothing—until we get more information," Lucy said.

"A cover-up!" Mike cried out. "If it wasn't Karen and you weren't in your do-as-Jesus-would-do phase, you'd jump all over this story. You'd have us running ourselves ragged digging out the facts!"

Mrs. Stegner nodded and said, "He's right, Lucy. I'm not sure you're being objective about this. Are you sure you're not protecting Karen?"

"I don't have to protect Karen. She wouldn't steal, it's as simple as that. But I'm not afraid of searching for the *truth.*"

"Newspapers aren't interested in only the truth, Lucy," said Mrs. Stegner. "They're interested in reporting the *facts*—as they emerge. If a bank gets robbed, you don't wait until you have the whole *truth* of what happened, you report what happened *when* it happened."

"But we don't even have all the facts, Mrs. Stegner,"

Lucy said.

"Then *what do you do next?*" she prodded.

Lucy hesitantly answered, "We investigate the story and assemble more facts."

"Right."

"But we won't print anything until we have them all," Lucy added as a qualifier.

"I'll go talk to Mr. Laker," Mike said enthusiastically.

Lucy looked surprised. "Mr. Laker?" she asked.

"Sure, he's in charge of the school finances. He has to know about it."

Lucy smiled knowingly. *Mr. Laker is the anonymous note writer*, she realized. *He's setting her up!* She looked at the faces of her co-workers and knew she couldn't tell them. But suddenly it changed everything for her. "You're in over your head," Mr. Laker had said to Karen.

The reporters took off with various ideas about tracking down the story, leaving Lucy and Mrs. Stegner alone.

"It's hard for you," Mrs. Stegner said sympathetically. "But this is what being an editor's all about."

Lucy nodded sadly. "I won't betray my friend."

There was a knock at the door. Mr. Felegy opened it and peeked in. "Sorry to interrupt," he said as he stepped fully into the room. Karen followed him, looking lost and helpless.

"What can I do for you?" Mrs. Stegner asked.

"It's what *Lucy* can do, actually," Mr. Felegy said. "We were wondering if she found the mysterious copies that Karen needs right now."

"Copies?" Mrs. Stegner asked.

"I haven't found them," Lucy admitted quietly. She spread her arms to Karen as if to say, *What can I do?*

Karen turned to Mr. Felegy. "I don't blame you if you won't believe me, but . . . I didn't take the money, Mr. Felegy."

Mr. Felegy shook his head. "Karen—"

Karen interrupted him: "At the council meeting tomorrow, I'll . . . I'll resign as president."

CHAPTER FOURTEEN

Joe Devlin gave his friends a few parting punches on their arms—just to remind them who was boss—and ducked into the woods. He followed the path through the bare trees as he always did at this time of day. He had to get home in time for dinner. His mom got angry when Joe was late, and Joe knew it was dangerous to make his mom mad.

The fallen leaves crunched under his leather boots. He liked the sound. It made him feel powerful, as if he were destroying entire cities under his feet like Godzilla in those Japanese movies. He marched on through the woods, unaware that he was being watched.

The trees suddenly gave way to a clearing, and, a few yards beyond, Joe heard the creek pouring over the time-worn stones. The wind kicked up, so he tugged the zipper up on his leather jacket. He made his way to the large tree that had conveniently fallen to bridge one side of the creek to the other. He had crossed it so often that he didn't think twice

107

about whether or not it was safe. He jumped on and strolled ahead.

When he reached the halfway point—identified by a rotted branch that stuck out of the side of the log—he heard a noise. It wasn't any of the familiar sounds he took for granted—the snapping of old bark from the tree, the creek gurgling below, birds singing somewhere in the forest—that made him stop and listen. This one was different. Joe waited, and it came again. It was the unmistakable sound of someone clearing his throat.

Joe turned around quickly and saw Matt standing on the bank behind him. Something rustled in front, and he looked to see Jack positioned on the bank ahead.

"Oh, it's you two," Joe said.

"Yeah, it's us," Jack answered.

Joe took a step forward but halted when Jack raised his hand. In it was a whip. Jack flicked his arm and, in turn, snapped the whip. It cracked loudly, scattering the birds in a nearby tree. Jack smiled, impressed with himself.

Joe squinted his eyes in a way he thought looked vicious. "Nice whip," he said. "Are you boys playing *Indiana Jones* this week?"

Matt, who was also holding a whip, cracked his as well, and Joe nearly lost his balance on the log from the fright. "My dad is a collector," Matt said.

"I'm happy for him," Joe said sarcastically.

"We've been thinking about it, Joe," Matt said. "We decided we're sick and tired of you bullying Oscar."

"Am I supposed to care what you think?" Joe said.

"You oughtta care right now," Jack said, "because you're not coming off that bridge until you promise to leave Oscar alone."

"Oh, yeah? What're you going to do if I refuse?"

Both boys cracked their whips.

Joe sneered at them. "You're pretty tough when it's two against one."

"And *you're* pretty tough when it's you and seven other guys against Oscar," Matt said. "Funny, but you're not so tough now."

"What're you going to do, whip me?" Joe challenged them.

"Worse than that," Matt said. "We're going to give you a bath."

"What?"

Jack continued, "If you don't promise to stay away from Oscar, you're going into the creek."

Joe nearly laughed at them. A dunk in the creek was nothing to him. "You think a little water scares me?"

Jack cracked his whip at Joe. Joe flinched and took a step backward. "Watch it with that thing!" he yelled.

"You probably don't care about the water yourself," Matt said. "But that leather jacket and those leather boots won't enjoy it very much. Water ruins leather, doesn't it?"

"It does if you're drenched in it," Jack said.

Joe realized what they were up to and looked stricken. "You clowns better not try it!" he threatened. "You ruin my jacket and boots and you'll pay for them."

"Why should we?" Matt asked. "You won't have any proof that we got them wet. You fell off the log on your way home."

"Besides, you probably bought them with the money you keep stealing from Oscar," Jack said.

"You force me into that water and you won't live to regret it!" Joe shouted.

Jack laughed and said, "What'll you do? Get your gang together and beat us up?"

"Count on it," Joe said.

"Yeah, but you can't always be with your gang, Joe," Matt countered. "Just like now. Whatever you do to us, we'll catch you alone and do back."

Jack cracked the whip again. "Y'see? You guys aren't the only ones who can play rough."

"On the other hand," Matt said, "all you have to do is promise that you'll quit bullying Oscar."

Joe spat at them. "I'm not making any deals with you sissies."

"I guess that's his answer," Matt said, and he cracked his whip at Joe again.

"Sounds like it," Jack agreed, and he flicked his whip at Joe, too. They were careful not to hit him, but he didn't know that. He moved first in one direction, then the other, struggling to keep his balance on the log.

"Promise?" Matt called out again as they slowly worked their whip ends closer to him.

"No!" Joe yelled back.

The two boys inched their whip snaps closer and closer. Jack got a little too close and hit Joe on the hand.

"Ouch!" Joe cried out. "That hurt!"

Jack was surprised but didn't show it. Having Joe in a state of fear encouraged him. "Now you know how it feels when you hurt other people," he said.

Joe paced like a lion between two tamers. His mind raced, trying to think of a way out—besides going into the water.

"Just promise, Joe!" Matt said.

Joe considered promising—and then going back on his word—but couldn't get the words out. It was galling to him to make any kind of promise to Matt and Jack. His pride wouldn't let him.

"That's it," Jack announced. "You're going in!"

Matt and Jack increased the flicks of their whips toward Joe. They had him dead center between them now. Joe looked down at the water and cursed loudly at the two boys. The whips cracked harder and closer until it seemed that Joe had no choice but to jump.

"Stop it! Stop it!" came a voice from the clearing behind Matt.

Matt didn't turn to look for fear that Joe might go for him if he did. "Who is it?" he shouted at Jack.

Jack and Joe both looked beyond Matt. Oscar rushed toward them, waving his arms and yelling. "Stop! Stop!" he cried out. He reached the end of the log on Matt's side and breathlessly said, "This is wrong. Don't do it."

Matt lowered his whip and said, "Oscar, listen—"

Joe started for Matt, but Matt was too quick. He flicked the whip at Joe to force him back.

"You just stay where you are," Matt said to Joe.

Jack shouted at Oscar, "Get out of here! We're trying to help you!"

"No!" shouted Oscar, red-faced. "This is wrong! What happened to your pledge? What happened to doing what Jesus would do?"

"Oh, brother," Joe mumbled. "I should've figured it was one of those religious things."

Matt said, "Jesus took action against the money changers, so *we're* taking action."

"It's the wrong kind of action," Oscar maintained.

"This is for *you,* you moron!" Jack shouted, clearly annoyed.

"If it's for me, then put your whips down!"

"Yeah, listen to him," Joe said.

"Be quiet," Jack growled and snapped the whip at him.

"It's *wrong!*" Oscar pleaded. "This *isn't* what Jesus would do. There are other ways to stop kids like Joe."

"Yeah, like what? Not speak to him?" Jack said sarcastically.

"Maybe. And maybe we're supposed to just put up with him, too. Maybe we're supposed to put up with him and even forgive him, just like God puts up with us and forgives us!" Oscar added firmly, "Now put your whips down and let him go!"

Matt wasn't ready to give in. "But he has to promise first!" he insisted.

"I don't want his promise!" Oscar cried out. "I don't want anything from him. I want you to let him go."

"No can do," Jack said. "I'm tired of his bullying everyone. If we can't do this for you, we can do it for someone else."

"Yeah, and then what?" Oscar said. "As soon as he gets away from here, he'll get his gang and hunt you down."

"Big deal," Jack replied. "Then we'll hunt *him* down. If he wants a war, he can have one. We have friends. We have kids who'll help."

Oscar waved a finger at him in accusation. "Then you'll be just like him—*bullies*. Is that what you want? You want to ignore your pledge to be like Jesus in order to turn into another bunch of bullies like Joe and his gang? Is that what you're telling me? Because if you do, then you'll have to give up friends like me and Lucy and Karen and the people at church! Don't you get it? This isn't the way to do it! Jesus had the better way! Now, are you going to put your whips down or not?"

Matt and Jack looked at each other, trying to make a silent decision. They both knew Oscar was right. Their hearts told them so.

"'Vengeance is mine,' says the Lord," Oscar reminded them. It was a verse they had seen the other night when they read their Bibles together.

Jack rolled his eyes, muttered under his breath, stepped

away from the end of the log, and slowly coiled up the whip.

"Ha!" Joe snorted and crossed the log. "I won't forget this," he said to Jack as he walked past. He sauntered away without looking back.

Jack and Matt glared at Oscar.

"It's what Jesus would do," Oscar said.

CHAPTER FIFTEEN

The funeral for Raymond Clark was a small affair held at the Chapel of Rest on the outskirts of Connellsville. Apart from Christine, her husband Robert, Whit, and Tom, there were three former co-workers from the printing company where Raymond had once labored and from which he'd been fired. It was hard for Whit to believe that only a few days had passed since Raymond Clark had entered his life. Now he was gone.

"Jesus said, 'I am the resurrection, and the life: he that believeth in me, though he were dead, yet shall he live; and whosoever liveth and believeth in me shall never die,'" the presiding minister read over the plain, brown casket. "The eternal God is thy refuge, and underneath are the everlasting arms."

He prayed a simple prayer about being comforted by God and looking beyond this life to the next one. "Help us to see the light of eternity," he concluded, "so we may find the grace and strength for this and every time of need. Through Jesus Christ our Lord. Amen."

Christine read a collection of psalms reminding them all of God's everlasting love. Robert, a tall, young man with dark, curly hair and wire-rimmed glasses, read passages from the New Testament about the peace of Christ and the never-failing love of God.

The minister then prayed, "Eternal God, who committest to us the swift and solemn trust of life, since we know not what a day may bring forth but only that the hour for serving Thee is always present, may we wake to the instant claims of Thy holy will, not waiting for tomorrow but yielding today."

That's what it's all about, Whit thought. *The days are so short, our time to serve God is so brief. Why do we spend so much time on things that don't really matter?* Whit echoed the words in his heart: "May we wake to the instant claims of Thy holy will, not waiting for tomorrow but yielding today."

The late afternoon was alive with colorful contrasts: the brown carpet of fallen leaves on the cemetery lawn, a cloudless sky, pale marble tombstones that glimmered orange in the fading sunlight. "Not a bad day to go home," Tom whispered to Whit at the grave site.

"Lord, have mercy," the minister said.

"Christ, have mercy," the small gathering replied. They said the Lord's Prayer together, and the minister said a few concluding remarks about God's compassion, then ended with, "The grace of the Lord Jesus Christ, and the love of God, and the communion of the Holy Spirit, be with you all. Amen."

Whit and Tom were formally introduced to Robert, then given heartfelt hugs from Christine. "Thank you for coming," she said tearfully. "My father had few friends here."

"I only wish we could have been better friends when it really mattered," Whit said.

Christine pulled Whit close and whispered in his ear, "You can let go of that now. It's finished. If you were really in the wrong, then consider it closed. My father forgives you. I forgive you. God has always forgiven you. What more do you want?"

"To follow Jesus," Whit whispered back, emotion rising in his throat. "But thank you for saying so, Christine. Bless you."

"Bless *you,* John Whittaker," she said.

Tom and Whit walked silently back to the car. After they climbed in and began the drive back to Odyssey, Tom asked, "So what now?"

"What do you mean?" Whit asked.

Tom stole a glance at his friend. "This whole experience is percolating inside you. I can tell. Where do you think it's leading?"

Whit shrugged. "That's what I keep thinking about. It'd be easy for me to feel guilty and start giving my time to every charity in town."

"You're doing that already," Tom pointed out. "Where in the world will you find *more* time to give?"

Whit shook his head. "I don't have any more time. So I have to prioritize the time I have. That's it, isn't it?"

Tom chuckled softly. That's what he'd been trying to tell his friend for weeks.

"You've been absolutely right, Tom," Whit said.

Tom looked surprised. "Really? About what?"

"About my time." Whit casually rubbed the top of the dashboard. "Jesus did His Father's work. That's why He said yes to certain things and no to others. Jesus knew how to prioritize. That's what you've been trying to tell me. I realize it now."

"Terrific," Tom said, impressed. "So where do you start?"

"The same place Jesus started."

Tom looked at his friend quizzically.

"Jesus often went off alone to pray," Whit said. "And that's exactly what I'm going to do."

****

Two hours later, Whit returned to Whit's End, where Oscar, Jack, and Matt were waiting on the porch. "Is it time for another meeting?" he asked as he opened the front door.

"We think so," Matt said. "If you have the time."

"I'll make the time," Whit said. It was dinnertime—a slow period for Whit's End's business. He let the three boys in, then closed the door behind them and locked it. He gestured to a table. "Sit down. Aren't Lucy and Karen coming?"

"We don't know where they are," Oscar said. "*Two of us* left school as soon as the bell rang in order to—" He stopped, then turned to Jack and Matt. "Maybe you should tell him."

Jack and Matt squirmed in their seats. Whit watched them curiously.

"Yeah, I guess we should," Matt finally said. "Go ahead, Jack."

"Me! Why do I have to confess?"

"Confess?" Whit asked.

"Oh, *I'll* do it," Matt said, and he told Whit what had happened with Joe at the creek. All in all, Whit was impressed with how well Matt told the story: He admitted fairly what he and Jack had done wrong and included what Oscar did right.

When he finished, Whit patted Matt's arm. "Well done, Matt," he said.

Matt shrugged awkwardly.

"Oscar, I want to commend you for the way you handled Joe," Whit said. "I think you're on the right track with him. Who knows? Maybe you'll lead him to Jesus eventually."

Oscar blushed.

"You two, on the other hand," Whit said to Jack and Matt, "should be ashamed of your behavior."

Matt slouched in his chair. Jack fiddled with a plastic spoon to keep from looking anyone in the eye.

"How did you *ever* think that threatening Joe with whips and trying to ruin his clothes in the creek was a good idea?" Whit asked.

Matt shook his head. Jack looked as if he might say something, then changed his mind. Instead he muttered, "Jesus did it."

"What Jesus did when He drove the money changers out of the temple was vastly different from what you did to Joe," Whit said. "Jesus was purifying God's holy place of worship. What were you two doing?"

"Trying to get Joe to leave Oscar alone," Jack said.

"Is that all?"

"Getting revenge," Matt admitted. He looked to Jack. "Come on, you know it's true. We wanted to get back at Joe for causing us so much trouble."

Jack nodded. "Yeah, I guess."

"Do you see what happened? You willfully distorted Scripture so you could vent your anger and get revenge," Whit said. He sighed deeply, then smiled. "Welcome to the human race."

Matt and Jack perked up as if they hadn't heard him correctly.

Whit continued, with deep understanding in his voice, "Boys, you did what some Christians have been doing for 2,000 years. You twisted the Bible around to suit your desires. It's sad but true. So let's learn from this mistake, all right? It's the Spirit within us that helps us to understand God's Word and leads us into the *right* action. We have to be very, very careful not to confuse our ideas of what Jesus would do with what we want to do. Do you remember what the apostle Paul wrote about the fruit of the flesh versus the fruit of the Spirit?"

They shook their heads no.

"Let's see if I can paraphrase what he said. It's in

Galatians, chapter 5. The fruit of the flesh is immorality, impurity, idolatry, *hatred, quarreling,* jealousy, *anger,* dissensions, envy . . . well, I think you get the idea. But the fruit of the Spirit is love, joy, peace, patience, kindness, goodness, faithfulness, gentleness, and self-control. See the difference? It's a good checklist when you're trying to decide whether you're behaving the way Jesus wants you to. Got it?"

"Yes, sir," Jack said.

"Would it be okay if we started over?" Matt asked.

"Start what over?" Whit asked in return.

"Our pledge," he replied, then nudged Jack. "From now on, we'll honestly try to do what Jesus wants us to do. Right?"

"Right," Jack said.

"Most of us have to 'start over' as Christians *every day,*" Whit said with a smile. They fell silent for a moment. Whit looked at the two empty chairs and said, "I wonder what happened to Karen and Lucy?"

****

"Why didn't you tell us about this before?" Karen's father asked her.

"I thought I could deal with it myself," she replied. Karen, her father and mother, and Lucy were in the Crosbys' living room. Somewhere a radio played soft guitar music. Karen and Lucy sat on the couch, facing Mr. and Mrs. Crosby, who nestled into two easy chairs. "I'm really, really sorry," she added.

Lucy felt awkward being there for this family meeting, but Karen wanted her nearby, if only for moral support. They had eaten dinner together, then moved to the living room to talk about Karen's troubles.

"Don't ever let things go so far before you talk to us," Mr. Crosby said as a final reprimand.

"Is there anything we can do?" Mrs. Crosby asked her husband as she reached over and gently took his hand. Mrs. Crosby was a beautiful woman with blonde hair and large, blue eyes who was once a model but had left the business to get married and raise a family.

Mr. Crosby was a handsome, easygoing man with friendly eyes, a ready smile, and plenty of jokes for Lucy. But he was deadly earnest now. "Without any proof, there isn't anything we can do about Mr. Laker," he said.

"What about the missing money?" Karen asked.

"Unfortunately, they have all the proof they need for that." He tilted his head and looked thoughtfully at the fireplace. The flames crackled and popped there. "I suppose we can refuse to pay the money, especially since you didn't steal it. But the school district won't sit still for that."

Mrs. Crosby rested her chin on her fist. "What if we refuse to pay and demand some kind of inquiry? Maybe that'll shake a few apples out of Mr. Laker's tree. If the money really is missing, he must've put it somewhere."

"It won't be an inquiry, darling. It'll be a *battle*," Mr. Crosby said. "Are we ready for that?"

"What would Jesus do?" Lucy asked them.

Mr. Crosby released his wife's hand to tend to the fire. He picked up a poker and jabbed at the logs a couple of times. "I get the impression from Scripture that it's better to be wronged than to fight or go to court. Jesus said it when He talked about turning the other cheek, and Paul wrote about it in First Corinthians."

"The truth is, Karen's reputation is solid," Mrs. Crosby said. "People who know her will also know she didn't steal the money. We can't worry about the rest."

"Then I'm right?" Karen asked. "I should resign from the student council?"

Reluctantly, Mr. Crosby nodded. "Yes, sweetheart. You probably should. Otherwise you'll spend the rest of the year battling this incident—trying to stay credible with those who are against you. Life's too short and you're too young for that."

"Do you mind?" Mrs. Crosby asked.

Karen considered the question. "Being president hasn't been so special, but I hate to quit like this. It's like admitting I'm guilty."

"I know, I know," Mr. Crosby said. "But unless you find those copies, there's nothing else you can do."

Lucy stood up. "I'm going home and ransack my house one more time."

"I'll look around here again," Karen said.

"Meanwhile, girls, I suggest we all do a lot of praying," Mr. Crosby said. He gave the fire one last poke, and it spat sparks back at him.

****

When Lucy got home, her mother informed her that Mrs. Stegner had called. Lucy slipped into the study and dialed the number her mother had scribbled on the pad. Somehow it felt very serious calling a teacher at home.

"Thanks for calling back," Mrs. Stegner said after they said their hellos.

"I was over at Karen's, talking to her parents," Lucy explained.

"No doubt they have a lot to talk about," Mrs. Stegner said. "I phoned to tell you that Mike's been working on an article about Karen's resignation. I assume she's still going to resign tomorrow?"

"Yes, ma'am."

The line hissed for a moment, then Mrs. Stegner said, "You're so close to this situation, Lucy, that I'm pulling rank on you. I'm making the decision to print an article about Karen's resignation and the allegations about the missing money."

"I figured you would," Lucy said.

"However, I want *you* to write an editorial. Make it a rebuttal if you want. But I want to print your response to what's happened. Will you do that for me?"

Lucy thought about the opportunity to set the record straight—or at least to try. "Yes, ma'am. Thanks for giving me the chance."

"I need it by tomorrow morning," Mrs. Stegner said.

"Okay," Lucy said. "I'll do my best."

"Thank you. And again, I'm sorry your friend is having such a hard time."

"So am I, Mrs. Stegner."

They said good-bye, and Lucy hung up the phone.

She glanced over at the cursor on her parents' computer as it sat indifferently on the desk. It winked at her over and over. *I'm going to have to write the best editorial of my life,* she thought.

CHAPTER SIXTEEN

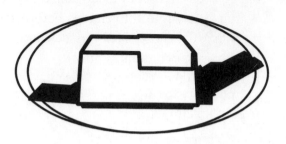

It was Judgment Day—or so Jack took to calling it later. The day began with Lucy and Karen meeting to pray together before school. They huddled outside next to a side door and asked God in hushed tones to be with them both, to give them courage to do what was right, and to allow the truth to come to light. It didn't seem like much to ask. But they both remembered Jesus' night in the Garden of Gethsemane, His betrayal at the hands of Judas, and the long road to that cross on top of the hill.

"Thy will be done," Karen whispered, and she meant it. At some point in the night, as she wrote her speech, she had felt her heart release the future. Whatever happened was God's business. It always was, she knew, but now she felt it deep in her heart.

Lucy had spent the night writing and rewriting her editorial for the paper. It was harder than she had expected. In one version, she told the whole story about the file and Mr.

Laker's misdeeds. She threw it away, though. Without proof, it was like bad gossip and would demean the good she'd hoped to do Karen. She wrote six versions before she settled on the one she liked the most. She was desperate to get it right for reasons even Karen didn't know.

"Are you coming to the meeting?" Karen asked.

"Only one reporter from the *Owl* is allowed to go to the student council," Lucy reminded her.

"That's silly. Whose idea was that?"

"Yours," Lucy said with a chuckle. "It was the first rule you got passed when you became president."

"Oh," Karen said, giggling. "Well, I'm *still* the president, and I say you can come in."

They both thought how nice it was to see the other smile. It felt as though it had been a long time since they had.

"I'll be there after I turn in my editorial to Mrs. Stegner," Lucy promised.

With a last hug for encouragement, the two girls went their separate ways: Karen to the library for the student council meeting, and Lucy to the *Odyssey Owl's* office. Only God knew where they would go from there.

****

Mrs. Stegner hadn't arrived at the *Owl* yet, so Lucy took out her editorial and set it on the table. She then took out another sheet of paper, looked it over one last time, and placed it next to the editorial.

It was her resignation.

As Lucy had asked herself again and again what Jesus would do with the *Owl,* she decided that He wouldn't go along with the hairsplitting between "truth" and "facts," between sarcastic reporting and honest news. Mrs. Stegner was a good teacher and had been more than fair to her, but Lucy felt it was wrong to teach kids that reporting was merely presenting facts without truth. Where was hope? Where was the belief that journalism could help lift people up rather than constantly drag them into the mud? The questions made Lucy feel tired, mostly because the answers weren't easy to figure out.

Maybe one day Lucy could start her own newspaper— one in which she would try to make telling the truth fairly and positively her highest priority.

She was about to leave when she suddenly decided that Mr. Felegy should see her editorial and resignation. Snatching them back up, Lucy went over to the storage closet to make copies. She turned the copier on and had to wait a few minutes while it warmed up. *It was only a couple of days ago,* she thought. *We were here making copies of Mr. Laker's file.*

"What did we do with those copies?" she asked herself, pressing the side of her head as if it might jog her memory.

Lucy placed the first page of her editorial on the glass, lowered the lid, and pushed the copy button. It hummed at her as the light flashed under the lid. A copy of page one slid out of the side and settled into the rack. She was about to put page two down when suddenly the machine stopped and a red symbol flashed.

"Out of paper," she muttered. Turning to the metal shelves behind her, she looked for packages of the right kind of paper. She knew from experience that putting in the wrong kind would jam the copier. "There it is," she said and reached up for the half-open ream. She caught the flap on the end and pulled the package toward her. It slid off the shelf and into her hands. A few pages dropped to the floor. She hated it when the kids were too lazy to close the half-open wrappers. They *always* lost a few sheets to the floor or under the cabinet.

Not this time, she thought and bent down to retrieve the fallen pages.

Lucy's hand was poised in midair, her fingers just about to touch one of the sheets, when she suddenly cried out.

****

"The meeting will come to order," Sarah Hogan announced after she'd called roll, fulfilling one of her duties as the clerk of the student council. Everyone was present and accounted for.

Karen sat in her usual chair at the front desk in the library. To her left was Brad O'Connor, the vice president. To her right was Olivia Bennett, the treasurer. Karen couldn't help but notice that neither of them would look her in the eye.

Along the wall next to the main library door sat Mr.

Felegy and Mr. Laker. Mr. Felegy watched her with a sad expression on his face. Mr. Laker's expression was cold and stony.

Not far from Mr. Laker, Mike sat with his notepad in hand. He didn't want to miss a word for the *Owl*.

No one in the room betrayed that they knew what Karen was about to do, but they all knew. Karen was sure of it. There was something about the stillness—the lack of the usual jokes from the usual kids—that told her they were waiting.

Karen decided to surprise them by going through their usual procedure. She stood up and asked, "Any old business?"

No one spoke.

"No old business? How about new business?"

Heather raised her hand and said, "Yeah. I want to hear you explain what happened to $347 of our money."

Karen felt wounded. She expected someone to attack, but not Heather, not someone who was supposed to be a good friend.

Is this how Jesus felt when Judas kissed Him? she wondered.

"We're checking into it," Karen said calmly. Why did she feel such a profound peace in the midst of this emotional hurricane?

"Who's checking into it?" Heather challenged her.

"I'll be working with Mr. Felegy to—"

"But aren't *you* responsible for the missing money?" Don

Kramer asked from the other side of the room. "You're the president. You were the one who took the money out, right? Isn't that what the sheet says?" He held up the financial statement.

Karen felt flustered. Did everyone get a copy of the statement?

Olivia Bennett waved at Don Kramer and said, "As treasurer, let me say—"

"We don't care what you have to say, Olivia," Heather snapped. "We want to hear what Karen has to say. We want an explanation. Rumors are flying all over the school that she stole the money."

Some of the rest of the council joined in, calling out for Karen to explain what was going on.

Karen held up her arms to quiet them down. "Look, it's confusing right now," she said. "The statement *looks* like there's money missing, but we're not sure there is."

"It says what it says," Heather pointed out. "How could the statement be wrong?"

Karen was stuck. She didn't want to mention Mr. Laker. It was pointless without any proof.

"What are you going to do about this?" Carol Cofield asked. "It looks pretty bad when the president of our council is accused of swiping—"

"I didn't swipe anything!" Karen shouted. "Who's spreading these rumors? Who passed out those statements? Why am I being accused without the benefit of the doubt? Something looks fishy, but it's not what you think."

"Then what is it?" Don called out.

Karen shook her head. "I can't say."

Someone booed her. She didn't look to see who. She didn't care. Someone else yelled "Cover-up," then booed as well. Then it seemed she was in front of a chorus of "boos" and "Cover-up!"

Do it now, she thought. *Resign before you start crying.*

"All right, calm down," she said. "Listen to me." The council quieted down. Karen stared at the top of the table, her eyes and face burning. Her well-rehearsed words stumbled forward. "Since I can't offer a good reason for the confusion about—"

"Confusion?" someone called out indignantly.

Brad O'Connor hit the table with his hand. "Let her talk, for crying out loud!" he demanded.

The room fell silent.

Karen looked at Brad out of the corner of her eye. "Thank you," she whispered.

"Go ahead," he said back to her.

"Since I can't offer a good reason for the confusion about that mysterious statement, and you guys obviously want to believe the worst about me—even though I've never done anything to betray your trust—I want to offer my res—" That was as far as she got. The tears filled her eyes, and her throat caught. She struggled to continue. "I want to offer my resignation, effective immediately."

She glanced up at the council through misty eyes, only to realize that they weren't listening to her. They were all facing the door. Karen hadn't heard the door open, nor had she seen Lucy enter with a handful of papers.

Everyone else saw it, though. It was like watching a silent movie. Lucy ran in, saw Mr. Felegy sitting next to the door, and frantically pushed the pages into his face. The kids didn't know what it meant. They had no idea why Mr. Laker suddenly went pale and nearly fell out of his chair.

The only thing any of them knew for sure—and could agree about when they gossiped for the rest of the day—was that Mr. Felegy stood up and dismissed them.

"This meeting has to be postponed," he announced. "Lucy, Karen, I'd like to see you in my office right away. You, too, Mr. Laker."

CHAPTER SEVENTEEN

"They're frauds," Mr. Laker said with a red face. He paced around Mr. Felegy's office impatiently, pausing only to scowl at Karen and Lucy.

Mr. Felegy looked over the bids for the report cards, the letter with its incriminating PS, and, of greater interest to him, the copy of the check for $2,000. "They look pretty genuine to me, Art," he said. "Where would these girls get the technology to put together forgeries?"

Mr. Laker grunted and said, "Kids can do everything with computers these days."

Karen and Lucy watched the proceedings silently. They both knew there was little for them to say. The evidence had to speak for itself.

"Are you telling me you've *never* received any money from Ballistic Printing?" Mr. Felegy asked.

"Well," Mr. Laker stammered, "what do you mean by 'received'?"

"Good grief, Art!" Mr. Felegy cried out. "Do you realize what this means? What about your retirement? Your pension?"

Mr. Laker abruptly turned to Karen and Lucy. "Get out!" he ordered.

The girls looked to Mr. Felegy.

"Thank you both for . . . er, all your help," he said. "I'll call you when I need you again."

The girls stepped out of the office and into the main office area. Mr. Laker slammed the door behind them. Maybe they imagined it, but the muffled shouts on the other side of the door had the sound of justice being done.

Mrs. Stewart looked at them warily.

Suddenly the door opened again, and Mr. Felegy said, "Mrs. Stewart, will you please get the district office on the phone?"

Mrs. Stewart's eyes bulged. "Anyone in particular?"

"Superintendent Murphy," said Mr. Felegy as he closed the door. Then he opened it again and added, "You'd better get someone from the legal department, too." He closed the door.

"This must be serious," Mrs. Stewart said excitedly as she picked up the phone.

Karen and Lucy looked soberly at each other. "It's serious, all right," Lucy said.

CHAPTER EIGHTEEN

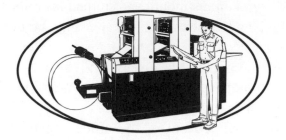

Whit dropped the newspaper onto the counter. "Well, what do you know about that?" he said. It wasn't the *Odyssey Owl* but the *Odyssey Times* he'd been reading. It chronicled the forced resignation of Mr. Art Laker and the school district's investigation of his business practices as school administrator over the past few years. The article also hinted at further investigations by the district attorney's office into Ballistic Printing and the many questionable "gifts" they had paid out to influential decision makers in Connellsville's and Odyssey's governments.

"You two really were in the middle of it, weren't you?" Matt said to Lucy and Karen.

"Yeah! You turned out to be the opener of a big can of worms," Jack said with a laugh.

"Please, Jack, I'm eating," Karen said as she scooped in a mouthful of ice cream.

Lucy smiled and said, "You should've seen Mr. Laker's

face when I walked in with those copies."

"I'll bet he nearly had a heart attack," Oscar said. He jammed a straw in his mouth and slurped his milk shake.

"Now I understand why you were so hesitant to talk to me about it," Whit said to Karen. "But where does that leave you?"

Karen swallowed her ice cream, then explained, "I'm still president of the student council. Mr. Felegy said he believes Mr. Laker juggled the numbers in our account to make it look like I'd taken the money."

"Mr. Laker was in a panic," Lucy said. "He was ready to do anything to keep Karen from being believed."

Whit nodded sympathetically. "He was so close to retirement. To be caught now jeopardizes his pension, his future, *everything*. It's sad, really."

"I'll feel bad for him later," Karen said. "Right now I'm too relieved to think about how he feels."

"What would Jesus do?" Whit asked.

"Forgive him, pray for him," Karen replied while she scraped the last of the ice cream out of the bowl.

"Will you?"

Karen replied while she licked the spoon. "Yeah. Probably. I made a promise, remember?"

"What about you, Lucy?"

"I resigned as the editor of the *Owl*," Lucy said. "But Mrs. Stegner wouldn't accept it. She said she needs me there."

"That's not *all* she said," Karen interjected. "She said that the school needed someone with Lucy's 'personal integrity' in charge of the newspaper. She's even going to let Lucy keep experimenting to make it more positive."

"To try to do what Jesus would do," Lucy said cheerfully.

"What about you boys?" Whit asked. "Do you have any new insights after all you've been through?"

The three of them looked at each other and shrugged.

"Typical," Lucy said, laughing.

"I'm gonna be honest," Jack said. "Following Jesus is tough. It's the hardest thing I've ever done, in fact. I don't know if I can do it. But I'll try."

"Me, too," Oscar said.

"All for one and one for all," Matt joined in. "I don't remember what verse that is."

Whit smiled and said, "*Three Musketeers*, I think."

"What are you going to do when Joe catches up with you?" Lucy asked them.

Jack grinned and said, "Turn the other cheek."

Matt began to laugh. "Joe's going to think we're crazy. First, Oscar won't talk to him, then he saves him from getting dunked in the creek. And if he tries to get revenge on us, we won't fight back! It'll drive him up the wall!"

The three boys laughed as only boys can about fighting. Karen and Lucy thought they were terribly immature.

"So it's a happy ending all the way around," Matt concluded.

Whit shook a finger at him. "Not a happy ending," he corrected. "This is just the beginning. We have a lot more challenges ahead of us."

****

"See ya, Oscar!" Matt called out.

Oscar turned to wave at Matt and Jack, then walked on up the street to his house.

"Shortcut?" Jack asked Matt, hooking a thumb toward the woods.

"Yeah."

They strolled down the path into the late afternoon shadows of the trees.

"It feels like snow," Jack said.

"It sure does," Matt agreed. "I'm going to have to dig my sled out of the garage. I think my dad's been using it to store paint cans on."

"I hate it when they do that," Jack said.

The sudden rustling of leaves and crackling of branches all around didn't give Matt or Jack time to react. Before they knew it, they were surrounded by Joe Devlin and his gang.

"It's payback time," Joe said.

"What would Jesus do?" Matt asked Jack.

As if to say "Come and get it," Jack spread his arms. "Turn the other cheek," he said.

Joe and his gang closed in on the two boys. But any enjoyment they might have had from their revenge was robbed by the maddening way Jack and Matt kept laughing.

****

Whit and Tom sat quietly at the counter of Whit's End later that night. Whit was about to lock the front door, but he enjoyed the silence of the building so much that he didn't want to move.

"It's nice when it's quiet like this," Whit said as he sipped his coffee.

"Yep," was Tom's only reply.

Whit glanced down at the newspaper again, then casually flipped the pages over. It didn't appear as if he were looking for anything special, but it turned out that he was. "Here it is," Whit said as he spun the paper on the counter so Tom could see.

It was an obituary for Raymond Clark. Christine had provided the newspaper with an older photograph of the man. He looked healthy and robust in the posed family portrait. Whit figured it was taken several years before, in happier times.

"Well, that's something," Tom said as he pointed to a line in the obituary.

"What?" Whit asked and peered over to look.

"It says here that he was an employee of Ballistic Printing until they laid him off a few months ago." Tom clicked his tongue. "Amazing."

Whit thought about it for a few moments. "What are we supposed to think about that?" he wondered aloud. "Ballistic Printing fired Raymond Clark, so he came to Odyssey, where he died. Because of him, we made promises to do what Jesus would do, which is why Karen decided to expose Mr. Laker rather than hide the truth—the truth about the very company that had fired Raymond Clark in the first place."

"It boggles the mind," Tom said. "Coincidence, you reckon?"

"I don't believe in coincidences. Just God."

EPILOGUE

It had turned into another hectic day at Whit's End. Whit didn't expect an ice cream shop to have a rush on a cold December day, but it was happening. By the time Tom Riley arrived with the crate from the dairy that Whit had asked him to pick up, Whit was serving a crowd of customers while trying to coordinate a Sunday school lesson on the phone with someone from the church *and* settle an argument between the two kids who were supposed to be setting up another Bible contest.

"Looks kind of busy in here," Tom said to Whit as he walked past the counter toward the kitchen. "Where do you want this?"

"The Mount of Transfiguration," Whit replied.

"What?" Tom asked.

"Sorry, not you, Tom. I'm talking to Marion at the church." He spoke more loudly into the phone, "I'll teach about Jesus on the Mount of Transfiguration." To Tom he said, "In the kitchen," then into the phone, "No, Marion, not the Mount of Transfiguration in the kitchen."

Tom put the crate just inside the door of the large refrigerator. He hesitantly returned to the chaos in the soda shop area, where Whit was now trying to make a chocolate shake with the phone still clamped between his shoulder and his ear, while Amanda and Bobby—the two organizers for the Bible contest—were at war.

"Help?" Whit mouthed to Tom.

Tom chuckled and asked, "When are you going to hire somebody to help you around here?"

Whit rolled his eyes. "I put the ad in the paper," he said, "but I haven't found the right person yet."

"Well, if I keep filling in like this, you're going to have to buy me one of those little aprons," Tom said as he stepped behind the counter.

"It's a deal!" Whit said. He hung up the phone, though Tom couldn't be sure whether Whit had finished the conversation or given up. He led Amanda and Bobby to one side to deal with their battle.

"What's wrong?" Whit asked.

"The Bible contest idea. It's boring," Bobby said.

With strained patience, Whit encouraged him to help come up with newer and more interesting ideas, but the boy didn't have any. He seemed content to simply complain about the *old* ideas.

"See?" Amanda said. "This is what I've been putting up with."

"Yeah, I know how it is," Whit said as the crowd of customers grew larger behind him. Tom struggled to keep up. Whit swallowed hard and asked himself, *What would Jesus do?*

He instantly thought of the time Jesus turned a loaf and a few fishes into a meal for 4,000 people. He also remembered how, after a bad day of fishing, Jesus sent the disciples back out in their boats and the nets nearly burst with their catch. *What would Jesus do with this chaos?* Whit wondered. *Jesus would perform a miracle and bring in someone to help!* came the answer. Whit then prayed silently, "Lord, do it. Give me a miracle."

Whit turned his attention back to Amanda and Bobby— cajoling them about keeping their sense of new ideas alive— when the bell above the door jingled and a new girl walked in. She was around 14 or 15 years old, with slender features, a pretty face, dark hair, and a newspaper tucked under her arm. Seeing the crowd, she nearly stepped back through the door, but she caught sight of Whit, Bobby, and Amanda standing nearby.

"Excuse me?" she asked politely. "Could you tell me how to get to Front Street?"

"North Front Street or South Front Street?" Whit asked. He considered his prayer from a moment ago as he eyed the girl.

She shrugged and said, "I don't know." Holding out the newspaper, she pointed to a "Help Wanted" ad for the Fashion Center on North Front Street.

"You're looking for a job?" Whit asked, his eyes lighting up.

"Uh huh," she nodded.

He took her hand in his and shook it. "My name's John Avery Whittaker. What's yours?"

"Connie Kendall," she replied.

Whit smiled and knew he had an answer to his prayer.

The epilogue is written with grateful acknowledgment to Phil Lollar and Steve Harris, writers of the "Connie Comes to Town" radio episode.

About the Author

Paul McCusker is producer, writer, and director for the Adventures in Odyssey audio series. He is also the author of a variety of popular plays including *The First Church of Pete's Garage, Pap's Place,* and co-author of *Sixty-Second Skits* (with Chuck Bolte).

Don't Miss a Single
"Adventures in Odyssey" Novel!

Freedom Run (#10)

When their Imagination Station adventure is cut short, Matt and Jack plead with Whit to let them return to the pre-Civil War South. But what awaits them is even more perilous than before! Through a whirlwind of events, the cast of *Dark Passage* is reunited for a treacherous journey through history along the Underground Railroad.

Dark Passage (#9)

When Matt and Jack discover a trap door in the yard at Whit's End, their curiosities get the best of them as The Imagination Station leads the pair back in time to the pre-Civil War South! And after Matt is mistaken for a runaway slave and sold at an auction, it's up to Jack to find and rescue him!

Point of No Return (#8)

Turning over a new leaf isn't as easy as Jimmy Barclay thought it would be. And when his friends abandon him, his grandmother falls ill, and the only kid who seems to understand what he's going through moves away, he begins to wonder, *Does God really care?* Through the challenges, Jimmy discovers that standing up for what you believe in can be costly—and rewarding!

Danger Lies Ahead (#7)

Jack Davis knew he was off to a bad start when he saw a moving van in front of Mark's house, heard that an escaped convict could be headed toward Odyssey, and found himself in the principal's office—all on the first day of school! Thrown headfirst into the course of chaos, Jack lets his imagination run overtime. Will it cost him his friendships with Oscar and Lucy?

The King's Quest (#6)

Mark is surprised and upset to find he must move back to Washington, D. C. He feels like running away. And that's exactly what The Imagination Station enables him to do! With Whit's help, he goes on a quest for the king to retrieve a precious ring. Through the journey, Mark faces his fears and learns the importance of obeying authority and striving for eternal things.

Lights Out at Camp What-a-Nut (#5)

At camp, Mark finds out he's in the same cabin with Joe Devlin, Odyssey's biggest bully. And when Mark and Joe are paired in a treasure hunt, they plunge into unexpected danger and discover how God uses one person to help another.

Behind the Locked Door (#4)

Why does Mark's friend Whit keep his attic door locked? What's hidden up there? While staying with Whit, Mark grows curious when he's forbidden to go behind the locked door. It's a hard-learned lesson about trust and honesty.

The Secret Cave of Robinwood (#3)

Mark promises his friend Patti he will never reveal the secret of her hidden cave. But when a gang Mark wants to join is looking for a new clubhouse, Mark thinks of the cave. Will he risk his friendship with Patti? Through the adventure, Mark learns about the need to belong and the gift of forgiveness.

High Flyer with a Flat Tire (#2)

Joe Devlin has accused Mark of slashing the tire on his new bike. Mark didn't do it, but how can he prove his innocence? Only by finding the real culprit! With the help of his wise friend, Whit, Mark untangles the mystery and learns new lessons about friendship and family ties.

Strange Journey Back (#1)

Mark Prescott hates being a newcomer in the small town of Odyssey. And he's not too thrilled about his only new friend being a girl. That is, until Patti tells him about a time machine at Whit's End called The Imagination Station. With hopes of using the machine to bring his separated parents together again, Mark learns a valuable lesson about friendship and responsibility.

Other Works by the Author

NOVELS:
Strange Journey Back (Focus on the Family)
High Flyer with a Flat Tire (Focus on the Family)
Secret Cave of Robinwood (Focus on the Family)
Behind the Locked Door (Focus on the Family)
Lights Out at Camp What-a-Nut (Focus on the Family)
The King's Quest (Focus on the Family)
Danger Lies Ahead (Focus on the Family)
Point of No Return (Focus on the Family)
Dark Passage (Focus on the Family)
Freedom Run (Focus on the Family)
Time Twists: Sudden Switch (Chariot/Lion)
Time Twists: Stranger in the Mist (Chariot/Lion)
Time Twists: Memory's Gate (Chariot/Lion)
You Say Tomato (with Adrian Plass; HarperCollins UK)

INSTRUCTIONAL:
Youth Ministry Comedy & Drama:
    Better Than Bathrobes But Not Quite Broadway
    (with Chuck Bolte; Group Books)
Playwriting:
    A Study in Choices & Challenges (Lillenas)

SKETCH COLLECTIONS:
Batteries Not Included (Baker's Plays)
Fast Foods (Monarch UK)
Drama for Worship, Vol. 1: On the Street Interview (Word)
Drama for Worship, Vol. 2: The Prodigal & the Pig Farmer (Word)
Drama for Worship, Vol. 3: Complacency (Word)
Drama for Worship, Vol. 4: Conversion (Word)
Quick Skits and Discussion Starters (with Chuck Bolte; Group Books)
Sixty-Second Skits (with Chuck Bolte; Group Books)
Short Skits for Youth Ministry (with Chuck Bolte; Group Books)
Sketches of Harvest (Baker's Plays)
Souvenirs (Baker's Plays)
Vantage Points (Lillenas)
Void Where Prohibited (Baker's Plays)

PLAYS:
The Case of the Frozen Saints (Baker's Plays)
The First Church of Pete's Garage (Baker's Plays)
The Revised Standard Version of Jack Hill (Baker's Plays)
A Work in Progress (Lillenas)
Camp W (CDS)

Catacombs (Lillenas)
Death by Chocolate (Baker's Plays)
Family Outings (Lillenas)
Father's Anonymous (Lillenas)
Pap's Place (Lillenas)
Snapshots & Portraits (Lillenas)

MUSICALS:
The Meaning of Life & Other Vanities (with Tim Albritton; Baker's Plays)
Shine the Light of Christmas (with Dave and Jan Williamson; Word Music)
A Time for Christmas
     (with David Clydesdale, Steve Amerson, Lowell Alexander; Word Music)